Obsidian Heart 2

Obsidian Heart 2

BY

TRACY WILSON

http://beautifulpublications.com

Published by
Beautiful Publications LLC
Stratford, CT 06614

This book is a work of fiction. Names, characters, places, and incidents are either products of the author's imagination or are used fictitiously. Any resemblance to actual events or locales or persons, living or dead, is entirely coincidental.

©Copyright 2021 Tracy Wilson

PRINT ISBN: 978-1-7343353-0-9
EBOOK ISBN: 978-1-7343353-3-0

Printed in the United States of America

Chapter 25

"Who is it?"

"It's me Sid..." Sid jumped up out the bed, snatched the door open, pulled me into his arms, and kissed me hard...

"My Queen... you're here..."

"Yes My King..." I breathed... "I'm here..."

"I'm sorry..."

"Shut up and kiss me again..."

"Yes My Queen..." he breathed as he held me in his arms and we continued kissing for a few moments... and then I stopped him...

"Sid..."

"Yes My Queen..."

"We need to talk..."

"Are you leaving me?"

"No..."

"Okay – as long as you're not leaving me – we can talk..." he said as he took me by the hand and led me over to the bed...

"Sid..."

"I know – you said we need to talk – I just wanted us to sit..."

"I need you to come with me to the bathroom..."

"Okay..." When we got in the bathroom, Sid began to smile... "Are we taking a shower?"

"Maybe later – but right now I need to pee..." I said as I opened my pants, pulled them down, and sat on the toilet...

"Umm... you're not peeing..."

"Go in my purse..." Sid took my purse, turned it upside down, and dumped everything on the counter. When he saw the pregnancy test, he got really excited...

"Oh my God!! You're pregnant?!"

"Open the test Sid!!" I laughed. I watched as Sid struggled to get the box open... "Put the test under me so I can pee on it..." Sid hurried over to me and put the test under me...

"Hurry up!!" he exclaimed...

"Okay, okay!!" I laughed as I started peeing...

"Are you done yet?!"

"Yes Sid – I'm done!!" I laughed. I got up, flushed the toilet and waited. Sid had his eyes glued to the test and I knew the test was complete when he started crying...

"Oh my God... My Queen... You're pregnant..."

"Yes My King... I'm pregnant..."

"You came here to tell me you want my child... and you want me..."

"Yes..."

"I love you so much..."

"I love you too..."

"Beautiee – we need to talk..."

"But I want you..." Beautiee breathed as she pulled Bazil into a kiss...

"I want you too... but we need to talk..."

"Can't I get some more first? Please?" Bazil couldn't resist...

"Oh Sid... Yes..." I moaned as the water beat down on us. Sid pulled me into his arms, pushed me back against the wall, and pushed his tongue in my mouth as he continued thrusting...

"Mmmph... Mmmph... Mmmph... Mmmph..."

"Hmmph... Hmmph... Hmmph... Hmmph... Hmmph..."

"Mmmph... Mmmph... Mmmph... Mmmph..."

"Hmmph... Hmmph... Hmmph... Hmmph... Hmmph..."

"MMMPH... MMMPH... MMMPH... MMMPH!!"

"HMMPH... HMMPH... HMMPH... HMMPH!!"

"Bazil... Don't stop... I'm cumming... I'm cumming..."

"I'm cumming with you..."

"HUH... HUH... HUH... HUH... HHHUUUHHH!!"

"UGGH! UGGH! UGGH! UGGH! UUUGGGHHH!!"

"Can... I... have... some... more?" Beautiee panted...

"We need to talk... and then I'll give you more..."

"What's wrong?" Beautiee asked as she propped herself up on her elbow..."

"Sit up..." Bazil sighed. Beautiee sat up along with Bazil and waited... "This is between you and me – okay?"

"Yes Bazil..."

"This doesn't go in the book – unless he tells you..."

"Ooohhh!! What happened?!"

"I have your word?!"

"Yes Bazil – you have my word – now tell me!!"

"What's in it for me?" he asked as he smiled mischievously..."

"Anything you want..." she answered as she smiled back at him mischievously...

"Anything?"

"Anything..."

"Okay – Sid came to see me..."

"Okay..."

"He went to his house to check the mail – Jade was upstairs...

"Ooohhh..."

"She called Smalls name..."

"WHAT?!"

"No – Smalls isn't fucking her..."

"Oh thank God!!" Beautiee exclaimed...

"Sid went upstairs and Jade was in the shower...

"Oh no – he fucked her?"

"She asked him to..."

"He could've said no!!"

"That's his wife..."

"And Amber is his Queen!!"

"So Jade tells him she's pregnant..."

"Oh my God!!"

"He tells Jade he'll be there for his child but he doesn't want to be with her - and since he met Amber, their marriage is over..."

"He shouldn't've fucked her..."

"That's what I told him..."

"But I understand..."

"You do?"

"Oh yea – I went crazy – remember?"

"Yes – I remember – I'm glad she wasn't pregnant..."

"Wouldn't've made a difference..."

"Really?!"

"Really!!"

"I shouldn't've asked..."

"Bazil – I love you – you're my life – but I'd be devastated if you got another woman pregnant..."

"I know – and here's the kicker..."

"What?"

"Amber might be pregnant too..."

"Oh hell no – that would never ever be me!"

"I know – and it may not be Amber either..."

"What are you saying?"

"He told Amber what happened – he told Amber his wife is pregnant – and she put him out..."

"She's not done with him..."

"That's what I told him..."

"Where is he now?"

"He's at the Holiday Inn..."

"I need to talk to him..."

"Beautiee – you gave me your word..."

"Yes I did – and I'm going to keep it – I won't put it in the book until he tells me..."

"Now that I told you what you wanted..." he breathed as he pulled her into a kiss... "I'd like to collect on what you promised me..."

"Have you decided what you want?"

"I'll give you a hint..." he breathed as he pushed her over on her stomach, climbed on top of her, and spread her cheeks...

"Let's get room service..." I suggested...

"Okay..." Sid agreed as he picked up the phone...

"How may I help you?"

"I'd like two orders – cheeseburger and fries – well done..."

"Okay – would you like dessert?"

"Sure – what do you have?"

"We have apple pie, cheese cake, and chocolate cake..."

"Two apple pies and two chocolate cakes..."

"Any drinks?"

"I pitcher of water will be fine..."

"Okay Mr. Heart – that'll be 45 minutes..."

"Okay – thanks..."

"How much time do we have?" I asked...

"We have 45 minutes..."

"Let's get in bed and see how many times you can make me cum!" I squealed as I hurried over to the bed, took off my robe, snatched back the covers, and jumped on the bed...

"Chandra?"

"Yes Chris?"

"Would you like to come with me to see Amber tomorrow?"

"Sure!"

"Good – we'll bring Maui – I need to bring Amber back her key – and it'll give me a chance to check on her..."

"I thought she was doing okay?"

"She was – until Sid slept with his wife again..."

"Oh no!"

"And get this – his wife is pregnant!!"

"Oh my God!"

"I know – right?"

"I don't know what I'd do in that situation..."

"It gets better..."

"What?"

"Amber might be pregnant too..."

"Oh my God – his wife and his mistress are both pregnant?"

"Probably..."

"I'm glad we don't have those issues Baby..." Chandra sighed as she pulled Chris into a kiss...

"I know that's right..." Chris breathed as she kissed her back...

"Room service!"

"Shit – Fuck – Don't stop Sid – I'm cumming again..."

"Ugh! Ugh! Ugh!"

"Room Service!"

"Give us a minute – we're cumming!" Sid growled...

"Haah... Haah... Haah... Haaahhh!"

"Ugh! Ugh! Ugh! Uuugghghh!"

"Okay..." I panted... "Now you can answer the door. Sid got up, put on his robe, went to answer the door, and when he did, I heard the guy laughing...

"Was it good?"

"Hell yea it was good!" Sid exclaimed...

"My man..." I heard him say...

"Thank you..."

"Charge it to the room?"

"Charge it to the room..."

"Have a good night..." Sid wheeled the table into the room and closed the door...

"Okay – I'm up..." I said as I got up and went to sit at the table...

"I'm so happy you're here..."

"So am I..."

"I know we need to talk..." he said as he took the cover off the food...

"Yes – we need to talk..."

"How many times did I make you cum?"

"Four or five – I'm not sure..."

"I liked it..."

"I loved it..."

"Can we do it again?"

"Yes..."

"So... about Jade..." he sighed as we started eating...

"What about her?"

"They won't let her have a baby in prison..."

"What would you do if your wife wasn't in jail?"

"I'd want to go to doctors' appointments and be there for her..."

"Exactly..."

"I don't understand..."

"I told you I didn't want to start anything with you until you were done with her – I told you I didn't want it to be the three of us – now that we're both pregnant – it's going to be the five of us..." I sighed...

"I'm sorry..."

"You don't have to apologize – she's your wife – she got pregnant by her husband – I just don't know how I'm going to deal with it..."

"I want to be there for my child..."

"That's not true..."

"Yes it is..."

"You want to be there for your child – but you want to be there for her too..."

"I'm sorry..."

"You don't have to apologize for wanting to do the right thing..."

"I have to tell her you're pregnant..."

"You don't have to tell her..."

"I don't want her to hear it from anybody else..."

"Okay – so you're going to tell her I'm pregnant – then what?"

"I don't know – I haven't figured that out yet..."

"Exactly..."

"I want to take custody of my child after he's born..."

"I'm going to have two children..."

"You're having twins?!"

"No – your wife will give birth first – you'll bring that child home – and then I'll give birth – and then we'll bring our child home – I'm going to have two children..."

"I love you so much..."

"I love you too..."

"I'm going to have a son and a daughter..."

"Your 1st born will be named Obsidian – your 2nd born will be named Prince – and if your 2nd child is a girl, she'll be named Princess..." Sid got up out the chair, got down on bended knee, and took my hand...

"Amber, My Love, My Queen – will you marry me?"

"Yes Obsidian, My Love, My King – I'll marry you..." Sid stood up, stood me up, picked me up in his arms, took me to bed, and gave me so many orgasms I lost count...

Chapter 26

"Good morning..." Sid yawned as he answered his phone...

"Sid – it's Smalls..."

"Yes Smalls?"

"Your papers were filed yesterday..."

"So I'm officially divorced?"

"Not quite..."

"What does that mean?"

"I had to make a revision to your agreement..."

"What happened?"

"Now that your wife is pregnant, I had to add a petition for custody to the papers..."

"Why would you need to do that – I'm the father!"

"It protects you both..."

"Protects us from what?"

"It protects you both from DCF getting involved because your wife is an inmate..."

"They get involved?"

"DCF always gets involved when an inmate gets pregnant..."

"Oh wow – do I need to worry?"

"No – your wife is willing to give you custody so there won't be any issues..."

"Thank you Smalls..."

"You're welcome – now we need to talk about your wife's settlement..."

"You had to revise that too?!"

"No – I just wanted to let you know I spoke with Bazil – you're all set..."

"I don't need to do anything?"

"Your wife gave me permission to act on her behalf so everything's been taken care of..."

"Okay..."

"Judge Dulberg is going to schedule a court date – you'll need to be there..."

"I will?"

"Yes – the judge needs to hear you both say you agree to the custody agreement..."

"Okay Smalls – keep me posted..."

"I will..." Smalls said as he hung up...

"Who was that?" I yawned...

"Smalls..."

"Everything okay?"

"Bazil gave me the money, Smalls is acting on my wife's behalf, he revised the papers to include a custody agreement, and I have to go to court so DCF doesn't step in and try to take my child..."

"Oh my God!"

"It's fine – they get involved whenever an inmate gets pregnant..." he said as he snuggled back down under the comforter and pulled me down with him... "Do you remember when I said I couldn't wait to hold you all day?"

"Yes... I remember..."

"Today is that day..." he breathed as he pulled me into a kiss and his phone rang again...

"This is Sid..."

"Sid – this is Marlowe..."

"Good morning Marlowe..."

"Your equity loan's been approved – you'll have the money in your account in 48 hours..."

"Thank you Marlowe..."

"You're welcome..."

"Have a good day..."

"Thanks Marlowe – you too..."

"Good news?" I asked...

"Yes..."

"You got the money!"

"Yes..." he breathed... "Now where were we?" he breathed as he kissed me again and his phone rang again...

"This is Sid..."

"Mr. Heart?"

"This is Mr. Heart..."

"This is Eileen from Allstate..."

"Yes Eileen?"

"Your claim's been processed – the check will be mailed today – you should get it in 2 or 3 days..."

"Thank you Eileen..."

"You're welcome – have a good day..."

"Who was that?" I asked

"That was Eileen from Allstate..."

"Good news?"

"My claim's been processed..."

"That's great!"

"Yes it is – now you can speak to the contractors, hire interior decorators, and do anything else you want..." he breathed as he kissed me again and his phone rang again. I giggled as he answered his phone...

"Hey Bazil..."

"Hey – you good?"

"I'm great..." he sighed...

"Aww – I'm happy for you..."

"Can I tell him?" Sid asked me...

"Yes – you can tell him..."

"Is that Amber?"

"Yes..."

"Sorry..."

"I'm not – she's pregnant!"

"Congratulations!"

"And we're getting married..."

"I'm really happy for you..."

"I'm happy too..."

"Did you speak to Smalls?"

"Yes – thank you..."

"You're welcome – and congratulations..."

"Thank you..."

"Can I tell Beautiee?"

"Yes Bazil..." Sid laughed...

"Good – 'cause I already told her about last night!" Bazil laughed...

"Bye Bazil!" Sid laughed as he hung up... "Let's try this again..." Sid breathed as he pulled me into a kiss and my phone rang... "I give up!" Sid laughed as I answered my phone...

"Hi Chris!" I laughed...

"You're laughing – that's good! How are you feeling?"

"Wonderful..." I sighed...

"Wonderful! You must be with Sid..."

"I'm pregnant!"

"Oh my God – congratulations!"

"And I'm getting married!"

"Sid proposed?!"

"Yes!"

"Yeessss!!"

"I'm glad you're happy..." I sighed...

"I'm glad you're happy!"

"I am Chris... I am..."

"Are you home?"

"No..."

"Well — I was calling to tell you we were going to stop by — but I guess that will have to wait until tomorrow..."

"Yea..." I sighed...

"Okay — we'll see you tomorrow..." Chris said as she hung up...

"Give me your phone..." Sid commanded...

"Yes My King..." I said as I handed him my phone. Sid turned my phone off, turned his phone off, put both phones in the nightstand drawer, and pulled me into a kiss...

"Now..." he breathed as he kissed me... "I'm going to spend the rest of the day holding you..." he breathed as he kissed me again... "As promised..." he breathed again as he pushed me on my back, got on top of me, spread my legs, and eased himself inside me...

"What happened?" Chandra asked...

"Amber's pregnant..."

"Oh wow..."

"I know..."

"I hope everything works out for them..."

"It will..."

"I'm glad she's happy..."

"Sid proposed..."

"Isn't he still married?"

"Not for long..."

"Amber said yes?"

"She said yes..."

"If she's happy – I'm happy..."

"I'm really happy for them..." Chris sighed...

"Good morning..." Beautiee sighed...

"Good morning – I brought you some coffee..." Bazil said as he handed her a cup...

"Thank you..."

"Guess what?"

"What?"

"Amber's pregnant!"

"WHAT?!"

"And Sid proposed!"

"Really?!"

"Yes!"

"This is like a fairytale with a happy ending – oh shoot – let me write that down!" Beautiee exclaimed as she put down her coffee, opened her nightstand drawer, and grabbed her pad and pen...

Chapter 27

"**Mmmm...** I don't wanna go..."

"We'll be alright..."

"I just want to block out the world a little while longer..." I sighed...

"I don't want to block out the world..."

"I need another day before I'll be ready to take on the world..."

"So..." he breathed as he kissed me... "We'll go home..." he breathed as he kissed me again... "And we'll take another day..."

"Might as well get ready..." I sighed...

"My Queen – you're not having second thoughts – are you?"

"No My King..."

"C'mon – let's go home...

"Jade Heart please report to the visiting area..."

"Smalls..." she sighed as she hurried to the visiting room...

"Good morning..."

"Good morning – why are you smiling?"

"Come with me..." Smalls said as he got up. Jade followed him to the attorney/client room and once they were inside, she pushed the door closed...

"Tell me!"

"Okay, okay – but I need you to sit down..."

"Alright – I'm sitting – tell me!"

"We go to court tomorrow..."

"So as of tomorrow, I'm officially divorced..." she sighed...

"Yes..."

"Oh well... it is what it is..." she sighed as she teared up...

"I'm sorry..." Smalls said as he got up from the table, went over to her, and put his arm around her to comfort her...

"Tell me why you were smiling when you came in here..." she sniffed...

"You got your settlement..."

"Oh..."

"I opened up an account for you at People's Bank downtown – your alimony payments will be deposited into your account – here's a debit card – you won't be able to keep it on you though – it'll be considered a weapon..."

"How will I get money out if I need it?"

"You go online to People's Bank – once you log in, you can transfer money from one account to another..."

"Another?"

"As an inmate, you have an account..."

"Oh so that's what they mean when they put money on the books..."

"Yes..."

"How do I set that up?"

"I already set that up for you..."

"Okay – how will I get my alimony?"

"I'll give Sid the account number so he can transfer the money every month..."

"Okay..."

"I have something else I need to talk to you about..."

"Okay..."

"I had to add a petition for custody of your child..."

"We don't need that – Sid's the father..."

"You're an inmate – anytime an inmate gets pregnant, DCF gets involved..."

"DCF? For what? I'm not an unwed mother – I'm not on drugs..."

"That's why I added a petition for custody..."

"I still don't understand why we need that..."

"You tell the judge you're willing to give custody of your child to Sid – Sid tells the judge he's willing to accept full custody – DCF doesn't have to get involved..."

"So my child will be raised by Sid and Amber..." she sighed...

"You can get visitation..."

"In prison?"

"You don't see children in the visiting area?"

"I do – but that's different..."

"Why?"

"Because the children are already born – or the mother is coming to visit the father..."

"So you don't want visitation?"

"Oh I want visitation – I can't be here for 12 years and not see my child!"

"Okay – I'll see you in court tomorrow at 9..." Smalls said as he got up to leave...

"Thank you..."

"You're welcome..." Smalls said as he left...

"What the hell was I thinking?" she sighed as she put her head in her hands...

As soon as I opened the door, the crystals, gemstones, and spheres came rushing down the hall and began circling around us...

"Sid look!" I exclaimed... They missed us!"

"I see!" he laughed as his phone rang... "This is Sid..."

"Sid – this is Smalls..."

"Hey Smalls..."

"We got to court tomorrow..."

"That was quick..."

"The judge wants to settle this as soon as possible..."

"So I'll be officially divorced tomorrow?"

"Yes..."

"What time?"

"9 a.m...."

"Okay Smalls – see you tomorrow..."

"Oh – one more thing..."

"Yes Smalls?"

"Jade wants visitation..."

"She wants me to visit her?"

"Not you – well – I guess you would be visiting her – to bring your child..."

"Jade wants me to bring our child to see her? In prison?"

"She wants to be in her child's life..."

"She will be – when she gets out of prison!"

"She's not willing to wait 12 years to see her child..."

"I don't know if I want to bring my child to prison every week to see his mother..."

"Can I make a suggestion?"

"Sure..."

"Go to court tomorrow – get your divorce – get custody of your unborn child – work out the visitation later – otherwise this will drag out indefinitely..."

"Can she really get visitation?"

"The only way she won't get visitation is if you petition the court to terminate her parental rights..."

"I'm not going to do that to Jade..."

"I didn't think you would..."

"I'll see you tomorrow..." Sid sighed as he hung up...

"What's wrong?" I asked...

"Jade wants visitation..."

"She wants you to visit her?"

"She's willing to give me custody of my child – but she wants me to bring the child to see her in prison..."

"Oh my God..." I sighed...

"I don't want to – but Smalls said the only way I can stop her from getting visitation is if I terminate her parental rights..." he sighed...

"This is exactly what I was talking about..." I sighed...

"I'm sorry..."

"Stop apologizing!" I snapped...

"I'm just trying to do the right thing!"

"We wouldn't be in this if she'd try and do the right thing..."

"What are you saying?"

"She wants visitation so she can see her child – that's only part of it..."

"I don't understand..."

"Every time you see her – your whole demeanor will change – and then you'll come home to me – and you'll be in a mood – and after you get settled and we get good again – it'll be time for you to bring the baby to jail – and as your child gets older –they'll be questions – why can't Mommy come out? Why can't Mommy live here – What did Mommy do – Why did Mommy do that – and those questions will have to be answered – and then our child will start asking questions – Oh God – I'm getting a headache..."

"Come here..." Sid sighed as he pulled me into a hug and held me...

"I thought you were going to get custody of your child – I thought we were going to raise our children together – I thought we wouldn't have to deal with any of this until after she got out of prison – Now she wants visitation – Now we have to be in prison with her..."

"I'm..."

"Don't say it!" I interrupted...

"I need to go out for a while..." he sighed...

"You're leaving?"

"I'll be back later..."

"Are you upset with me?"

"No..."

"Then why are you leaving when we just got home?"

"I have something I have to do..." he answered as he let go of me and went down the hall. I watched as the crystals, gemstones, and spheres followed behind him and laughed to myself...

Chapter 28

"Hey Sid..." Bazil answered...

"Hey..."

"What's wrong?"

"Can you meet me at Andinis?"

"We drinkin'?"

"Yea..."

"I'm on my way..."

"Beautiee – I'm going to meet Sid at Andinis – I'll see you later tonight..." Bazil said as he got up to leave...

"Mr. Osgood?"

"Yes Mrs. Osgood?"

"Lock the door..." Bazil did as he was told...

"Come here..." Bazil went over to her and pulled her into a kiss...

"Don't keep me waiting too long..."

"I won't..." he breathed as he kissed her... "I promise..."

"I'll see you tonight..."

"See you tonight..." Bazil said as he let go of her, unlocked the door, and left...

"Guard?"

"Yes Jade..." Gertrude answered...

"Can you take me to the infirmary?"

"Are you having a medical emergency?"

"No – but I need to speak to the nurse..."

"C'mon..." Gertrude sighed as she took Jade by the arm and escorted her to the nurse...

"Hi Jade – how are you feeling?" the nurse asked...

"What's your name?"

"Donna..."

"Hi Donna..." Jade sighed...

"Jade... what's wrong?"

"I'm thinking about having an abortion..."

"Why?"

"Does it matter?"

"No – I just thought you might wanna talk..."

"I go to court tomorrow..."

"Ohh..."

"After tomorrow, I'll be officially divorced..." she sniffed as she started crying...

"Oh Jade..." Donna said as she put her arms around Jade to comfort her...

"My husband's going to take custody of our baby after he's born – I can't go 12 years without seeing my child – especially because he'll be raising our child with his Queen!" she snapped...

"His Queen?"

"The Bitch he left me for – he calls her his Queen..."

"Ohh..."

"My attorney says I can get visitation – but I don't want my ex-husband to bring our child to see me – and then take him away..."

"I know what you mean – it breaks my heart when I see one parent dragging their kids kicking and screaming because they don't want to leave the other parent..."

"Exactly..."

"How much time did you get?"

"12 years..."

"So your child will either be pulled back and forth between the three of you – or you won't see your child at all for 12 years..."

"Exactly – and when my child asks Mommy why she's in jail, I'll have to explain Mommy's in jail for trying to kill your other Mommy..."

"Oh shit – is that true?"

"Yea..."

"Okay – you don't have to make a decision today – but we can go over the options...

"Thanks for coming..." Sid sighed...

"What's wrong?"

"I don't know where to start..."

"Start at the beginning..."

"Welcome to Andinis – nice to see you again Mr. Osgood – right this way..." the hostess said as she took them to the table... "The waitress will be here to take your orders – we have some new items on the menu..." the hostess said...

"Hello Mr. Osgood – nice to see you again..." Carmen said as she came over to the table... "May I start you off with some appetizers?"

"Yes – we'll have Risotto Balls, Veal Meatballs, Rabe & Sausage, Fried Calamari – and two Samuel Adams..."

"Okay – I'll be back with your drinks and appetizers..." she said as she went to place the order...

"What happened between tonight and this morning?"

"Last night was everything..." Sid sighed...

"Sounds good..."

"First of all – Amber tells me she needs me to help her in the bathroom – so I asked her if we were taking a shower – she says maybe later – I need to pee..."

"Sounds just like Beautiee..." Bazil laughed...

"So Amber tells me to go in her purse and she has a pregnancy test in there – I asked her if she was pregnant and she tells me to open the test and put it under her so she could pee on it!" Sid laughed...

"Sounds like something Beautiee would do..." Bazil laughed...

"That's how she told me she was pregnant..."

"Aww..."

"Here are your appetizers and your beers..." Carmen said as she placed them on the table... "Can I get you refills?"

"No thank you..." Sid said...

"If you need anything else – I'll be over there..." she said as she walked away and they continued...

"So – Amber says let's order room service – she asks me how much time we have before the food comes – I tell her 45 minutes – she says let's get in bed and see how many times you can came me cum before the food gets here..."

"My man!" Bazil exclaimed as they high-fived...

"Next thing you know – Room Service! – but we're about to come so I'm yelling – give us a minute – we're coming!"

"I swear – Beautiee and Amber must've been sisters in a past life!" Bazil laughed...

"So we're eating, we're talking, and I tell Amber I want to take custody of my child – and..." Sid couldn't finish...

"Sid..." Bazil whispered as Sid got choked up...

"She says we're going to have two children..."

"I knew she'd accept your child..." Bazil sighed...

"That's when I proposed..."

"That's beautiful..." Bazil said...

"I got the room for two nights – I thought she'd need some time to get over what happened – but when she showed up to let me know she was pregnant – I can't lose her..." Sid sighed as he started tearing up again...

"Okay – when did shit go left?"

"After Smalls called me..."

"What happened?"

"We go to court tomorrow..."

"That's good..."

"Jade wants visitation..."

"She wants you to visit her?"

"She wants me to bring my son to see her in prison – she's not willing to wait 12 years to see our child – Smalls said I should just show up tomorrow, get custody, and worry about visitation later so this doesn't drag out – and Amber isn't trying to hear it..."

"I'm sorry..."

"That's another thing – she told me to stop apologizing!"

"Damn – everything was going so good – does Jade know Amber's pregnant?"

"Hell no – not yet..."

"Don't tell Smalls!"

"I'm not – but Amber got so upset – I left..."

"Sid! That's the worst thing you could've done!"

"I didn't know what else to do – I told her I'm just trying to do the right thing – I tried to apologize - she wasn't trying to hear it – she said every time I see Jade my whole demeanor will change – and then I'll come home to her – and I'll be in a mood – and after I get settled and we get good again – it'll be time for me to bring the baby to jail – and as my child gets older –they'll be questions – why can't Mommy come out? Why can't Mommy live here – What did Mommy do – Why did Mommy do that – and those questions will have to be answered – and then our child will start asking questions – and then she said she was getting a headache – I tried to comfort her – and she just kept going!"

"Sid – she has a right to be upset – and you need to understand that..."

"She said she thought I was going to get custody of my child and we were going to raise our children together – but now she feels like we'll be in prison with Jade..."

"You shouldn't've left Sid – that sends a message that you don't care how she feels – you don't ever wanna do that – especially now that she's pregnant – trust me – I know – I went through it with Beautiee..."

"You did?"

"Oh yea..."

"How'd you get past it?"

"You remember when I told you she locked me out of the guest room and I took the door off the hinges?"

"Yea..."

"Well – I left a letter on the bed for her – I poured my heart out to her – we both got emotional and we both cried..."

"Did that work?"

"It wasn't about me trying to get my letter to work – I'd do anything to keep from losing her – I wrote her a letter because I couldn't bring myself to tell her how I was feeling..."

"Wow – that's deep..."

"Amber needs to know that she can speak her mind and vent to you · and you need to make her feel it's safe for her to do that..."

"I have an idea – and I need your help..."

"What do you need?"

"I'm going to take my gemstones that my great-grandmother passed down to my grandfather, my father, and now to me – and I'm going to take them to Kay Jewelers and have two custom wedding bands made for us with the gemstones..."

"Oh wow... okay Sid... I see you..."

"Do you think that will work?"

"Wrong question..."

"Do you think that will show Amber how much I love her and how much she means to me?"

"Yes..."

"Okay – I'm ready to go!" Sid exclaimed as he went to pay the check..."

"Thank you - Mr. Osgood – always a pleasure..." Carmen said...

"You're welcome – I'll see you again..." Bazil said as they left...

"Welcome to Kay Jewelers – I'm Winston – how may I help you today?"

"Hello Winston – I'm Bazil and this is Sid – Sid needs your help..."

"How can I help you?" Winston asked...

"I have 23 gemstones that have been passed down to me from my great-grandmother, to my grandfather, to my father, and now to me – I'd like to put the stones into two custom-designed wedding bands for me and my fiancée..."

"Let me show you what we have..." Winston said as they followed him over to the show case...

"I want this one!" Sid exclaimed...

"Aaahh... you like White Gold I see..."

"I like the style – I think the stones will look great in that setting..."

"That's our Tungsten Carbide – it holds 12 to 15 stones – the great thing about this band is that it's for men and women - are you getting the same band for your fiancée?"

"Yes..." Sid answered...

"Do you have the stones with you?"

"Yes I do..."

"May I see them?"

"Of course..." Sid said as he took the box out his pocket and handed it to Winston..."

"Oh my – these are exquisite..."

"Thank you..."

"I'll take good care of them..."

"I know you will..."

"Do you know how you'd like them designed?"

"Yes – for my band – I want 5 stones in the middle – I want the small Amethyst in the middle - and two Garnets on each side – for her band I want the larger Amethyst in the middle and two Garnets on each side..."

"Okay – how would you like the other stones?"

"For my band I'd like Blue Topaz, Peridot, Green Brazilian Flourite, Labradorite, Lemon Quartz, Tanzanite, and Carnelian – for her band I'd like Citrine, Fluorite, Blue Topaz Baguette, Labradorite, Ametrine, and Clear Quartz..."

"You wouldn't happen to have written that down by any chance – would you?"

"I did..." Sid said as he handed Winston the paper...

"Oh thank God!" Winston laughed...

"How long will this take?"

"I'm not sure – it may take a week or so...

"That's fine..."

"Will you be getting them engraved?"

"Yes – but I want to wait until we set a date..."

"That's fine – you can just set a date now – and then I can have them engraved before you come pick them up..."

"Okay – I'll do that..."

"Do you have a preference as to the order of the other stones?"

"No..."

"Okay – what size are you?"

"I'm a size 13..."

"What size is your fiancée?"

"She looks like a size 7..."

"We can always resize it – you picked a wide band so it won't interfere with the stones..."

"Thank you Winston..."

"You're welcome ‑ do you have an account with us?"

"No..." Sid answered...

"I'll get you an application..." Winston said as he started to walk away from the counter...

"I don't want an account – I'll use my credit card..." Sid said as Winston ignored him and went to get an application. When he came back he put the application in front of Sid...

"Just sign here and give me your driver's license – I'll fill in the rest..."

"Winston – I don't want an account..."

"Yes you do..."

"Winston..."

"Sid – let me explain to you why you need this card..."

"Okay..."

"Once your application is approved – you get 25 percent off for opening an account – and you'll also get $50 off for every $500 you spend..."

"Okay..."

"You can pay the balance off in twelve months with no interest if you like..."

"Okay – that's fine..." Sid said as he placed his driver's license on the counter..."

"Your name's Obsidian Heart? As in Heart Tech?"

"Yes..."

"Oh wow – I had no idea – it's a pleasure to meet you!" he said as he grabbed Sid's hand and shook it...

"Nice meeting you too..."

"I'll be right back!" Winston exclaimed...

"He seems really excited..." Sid laughed...

"He is — you're going to get a nice line of credit — he's going to get a nice commission..." Bazil laughed...

"Ohh..." Sid laughed...

"Mr. Heart — you've been approved — your credit line is $50k..."

"$50k?"

"Yes sir!"

"Thank you Winston..."

"You're welcome — would you like me to add your fiancée's name to the account?"

"I'll come back and add my wife to the account after we're married..." Sid answered...

"Okay — I'll call you in a few days — don't forget — call me with a wedding date so I can have your rings engraved..."

"We will — talk to you soon..." Sid said as they left...

"I'm going to do a pelvic exam and an ultrasound — we'll take it from there — you don't have to do anything today — okay?"

"Okay..." Jade sighed...

"Okay — I need you to get undressed from the waist down..."

"Okay Jade said as she got up off the table, took of her jumpsuit, put on the gown, and got back up on the table..."

"Okay — scoot down a bit so I can see what's going on..." Jade scooted down and she proceeded with a quick pelvic exam — by the time she felt Donna's fingers inside her she was finished...

"Wow – that was quick..."

"Everything feels okay – now let's see how everything looks..." she said as she squirted the gel on Jade's stomach, turned on the machine, and started doing the sonogram... "Hmmm..."

"Is everything okay?"

"It's hard to tell what's going on – I need to do a transvaginal ultrasound..."

"What's a transvaginal ultrasound?"

"I'm going to put this long tube in your vagina – it will help me see your uterus, fallopian tubes, ovaries, cervix, and your vagina..."

"Will it hurt?"

"No – it doesn't use radiation – you might feel a little discomfort as I'm putting the transducer in, but that's it..."

"Okay..."

"Are you ready?"

"Yes..."

"Take a deep breath... then relax..." she said as she put the transducer in her vagina... "Look... see that tiny little peanut right there?"

"Yes... I see it..."

"That's your baby..."

"I know..." Jade whispered as she started crying...

"Do you want a picture?"

"Yes..." she sniffed...

"Okay... I'll print one out for you..." Donna said as she printed the picture for her...

"Can I get up now?"

"Yes Jade — I'm finished..." she answered as Jade got down off the table and put her jumpsuit back on...

"How far along am I?"

"I'd say you're about 2 months..."

"Okay..." Jade sighed...

"Okay — now we need to talk about the abortion..."

"Okay..." Jade said as she started tearing up...

"There are two categories of abortion..."

"Okay..." Jade said as tears ran down her cheeks...

"Medical is where we use medication that causes the uterus to expel the pregnancy. Surgical is where the clinician removes the pregnancy. The Medical Abortion uses a pill — it's similar to a miscarriage — you cramp, there's heavy bleeding, it can take longer, and requires more appointments..."

"Oh my God... I can't..." Jade whispered...

"The Surgical Abortion feels more invasive, has more pain management, and is available quicker with fewer appointments. If you decide you want to go through with an abortion, you'll receive information on both procedures that explains the side effects and consequences.

Before you get the abortion, both procedures require an education session and counseling..."

"I don't need education or counseling..." Jade said...

"Jade... it's mandatory..."

"Okay..."

"Let me know what you decide to do..."

"Okay Donna – thanks..."

"Gert – she's ready..." Gertrude came into the nurses' area and took Jade by the arm...

"C'mon..." she sighed as she took Jade back to her cell...

Chapter 29

"**Good** morning My Queen... Sid breathed as he kissed me...

"Is it?" I asked as I got up out the bed...

"I'm..."

"You're sorry – right?!" I interrupted...

"Yes..." he sighed...

"Do you know why you're sorry or do you just say you're sorry out of habit?!"

"Please – let me explain..."

"I swear to God – you better not be telling me you slept with Jade again..."

"This isn't about Jade..." he said as he followed me down the hall to the living room... "This is about me..."

"Let me get some coffee first..." I sighed as I went into the kitchen. Sid watched me make the coffee without saying anything. After I made the coffee, I handed him a cup and sat down next to him...

"I went to see Bazil last night..."

"You said you had to go because you had something to do!"

"I did..."

"What did you have to do with Bazil — especially after we just got home?!"

"I didn't know how to comfort you yesterday..."

"You were comforting me just fine when we were at the hotel..."

"I know — but after Smalls called me yesterday — you got so upset — I tried to apologize — you didn't want to hear it..."

"I don't want to hear you say you're sorry - I want you to hear me!"

"I know that now — and that's why I'm sorry..."

"I don't want to hear it!!" I said as I put my hand in his face and then I pulled him into a kiss...

"I love you..."

"I love you too..." I looked up and noticed the crystals and spheres glowing and spinning... "Sid?"

"Yes My Queen?"

"Where are the gemstones?"

"What time is it?"

"It's 7:30..."

"We need to get ready – we have to be in court by 9..."

"We?"

"Yes..." he answered and then he stood up, took my hand, and pulled me towards the bathroom...

"Good morning..." Smalls greeted...

"Good morning Smalls, good morning Jade..." Sid greeted. Jade didn't respond...

"Good morning..." I sighed as we went inside. I was starting to think I should've just stayed home. When we got in the court room I went to sit in the back...

"Amber – come with me..." Sid said...

"I don't think that's a good idea..." Smalls said...

"Smalls..." Sid started to say...

"It's fine Sid – I'll sit back here..." I sighed...

"Okay..." Sid said as he went to the front of the court room with Smalls and Jade...

After Smalls sat down the Bailiff spoke:

"All rise." We all stood up. "Department One of the Superior Court is now in session. Judge Dulberg presiding. Please be seated."

"Calling the case of Jade Heart versus Obsidian Heart. Are both sides ready?"

"Ready Your Honor..." Sid answered...

"Ready Your Honor..." Smalls said.

"Let's start with the divorce..."

"Your Honor?" Jade asked as she stood up...

"Yes Mrs. Heart?"

"I'd like Amber to leave the courtroom..." she said as she turned and pointed at me...

"Ms. Morrison – please leave the courtroom..." I was already on my way out the door before the judge finished his sentence...

"Let's try this again..." the judge sighed... "We're here to discuss the particulars of the divorce first..."

"Yes Your Honor..." Smalls acknowledged...

"Mrs. Heart – you've agreed to a settlement of $500k, plus alimony of $1,000 a week for 12 years..."

"Yes Your Honor..." Jade acknowledged...

"Mrs. Heart – your husband's company is worth a lot of money – are you sure you want to settle for only $500k?"

"Yes Your Honor..." she answered...

"So noted – now let's settle the custody of your unborn child..."

"That's already been settled..." Sid said...

"Mr. Heart – please refrain from addressing me until you're called to speak..."

"Yes Your Honor..."

"Mrs. Heart – according to this petition – you've agreed to give your husband full custody of your unborn child – is that correct?"

"Yes Your Honor..."

"Would you like to petition the court for visitation at this time?"

"I'm not sure..."

"Very well – I'll enter a judgement granting the divorce between Obsidian Heart and Jade Heart. Custody of the unborn child will be granted to Mr. Heart. Mrs. Heart will be given an opportunity to petition the court for visitation after the child is born..."

"Thank you Your Honor..." Jade said...

"Mr. Heart..."

"Yes Your Honor?"

"You're officially divorced. You've agreed to a settlement of $500k and $1,000 a week in alimony for 12 years. You'll receive full custody of your child – however – Mrs. Heart can petition the court for visitation – and let me make this clear – I will grant her visitation..."

"Yes Your Honor..." Sid acknowledged...

"Smalls – I need to see your client in my chambers..." he said as he got up from the bench and went in his chambers...

"Why does he want to see me in his chambers?" Jade asked...

"I don't know..."

"Can you be in there with me?"

"I can let the judge know you want me to be present if you want..."

"Okay..." Smalls took Jade to the judge's chambers and knocked on the door...

"Your Honor?"

"Yes Smalls – come in..."

"Your Honor – my client has requested that I come with her..."

"Ms. Heart – I'd like to speak with you privately – if you don't like what I have to say – you can leave..."

"Can my attorney wait for me?"

"Absolutely..."

"I'll be in the court room..." Smalls said as he left Jade in the judge's chambers and went back to the court room...

"What's going on?" Sid asked...

"I have no idea..." Smalls sighed...

"Ms. Heart – please – have a seat..."

"Okay..."

"12 years is a long time..."

"Yes Your Honor – it is..."

"Please – call me Joel..."

"Okay... Joel..."

"May I call you Jade?"

"Sure..."

"Jade..." he sighed as he got up, went to sit by her, and took her hand...

"Yes Joel?"

"I want to make your time in prison easier..."

"Easier?"

"I can have you transferred to a section where you can be more comfortable... I want to be able to come visit you... I've grown feelings for you..."

"Are you fucking kidding me?!" she snapped as she pulled her hand away from him...

"Jade – did I say something to offend you?"

"You're offering to make my stay more comfortable – as long as I agree to be your whore – and you don't think that's offensive?!"

"Jade – you have me all wrong..." he said as he got down on bended knee in front of her and took her hand... "I'm not asking you to be my whore..."

"I'm sorry – I just thought – never mind – I feel so stupid..."

"Jade Heart..." he sighed as he reached in his pocket and pulled out a velvet box...

"Oh my God..." she whispered. Joel opened the box and showed her the ring...

"Will you marry me?"

"Are you sure you want to marry me?"

"I've never been more sure of anything in my life..."

"Come sit..." Jade said as she patted the chair. Joel closed the box, got up off his knee, and sat down beside her... "Why me?"

"I've been on the bench for 30 years – I'm not getting any younger – and I'm not trying to meet someone and start dating again just to have my heart broken..."

"How do you know that will happen?"

"I don't – and I'm not trying to find out..."

"Joel – I'm flattered – but I just got divorced – I'm pregnant – I don't know what I'm going to do yet..."

"You don't have to have sex with me if you don't want to – I can wait until you're ready to be intimate..."

"I don't think I'll ever be ready to be intimate as long as I'm in prison..."

"12 years is a long time to be alone... and it's even longer when you're lonely..."

"This is a lot – I had no idea you had feelings for me..."

"I do..."

"How are you going to be able to be a judge and be married to an inmate? What will your colleagues think?"

"I don't give a damn what my colleagues think – once we get married – I'm leaving the bench..."

"You'd leave the bench? For me?"

"If you say yes... then yes..."

"And you're willing to accept my child?"

"Of course..."

"I need to think about this..."

"So... are you saying maybe?"

"I'm saying maybe..."

"Can I kiss you?"

"Yes Your Honor – I mean Joel..." Joel took Jade's face in his hands and kissed her gently and she started crying...

"Please... don't cry Jade..."

"I'm crying because I'm happy..."

"That's fine with me..."

"So how does this work?"

"Well – once you agree to marry me – you come back here – and we can get married in the court room – or in the judge's chambers..."

"You're going to perform your own wedding?"

"No – I'm going to ask Harland Duffey..."

"I still need to think about it..."

"Okay – I'll give you some time..."

"Can I tell Smalls?"

"Not yet..."

"Why?"

"I want you to wait until you say yes..."

"Okay... I'll wait..."

"Can I visit you?"

"Yes Joel..."

"Okay – you can go back in the court room – oh – one more thing..."

"Yes Joel?"

"When we go back in the court room – call me Your Honor..."

"Okay..."

"They've been in there a while now..." Sid said...

"I know..." Smalls acknowledged...

"You sure you don't know what's going on?"

"I have no idea – here they come now..." Smalls said as he stood up a long with Sid...

"Smalls – you can take your client back to prison – have a good day..."

"Thank you Your Honor..." Smalls said as the judge got up and went back into his chambers... "Jade – what was that all about?"

"Nothing..." she sighed...

"Goodbye Jade..." Sid said...

"It certainly is..." Jade sighed as Sid left the court room...

Chapter 30

"Hey..." I sighed when I saw him...

"Hey..." he sighed as he pulled me into a hug...

"What's wrong?"

"Sid – I gotta run – you'll get a copy of the court papers in a few days..." Smalls said as he took Jade by the hand and led her to his car...

"What happened in there?" I asked...

"I'll tell you when we get where we're going..." he answered as he took my hand and pulled me towards the car...

"Thanks Smalls..." Jade sighed...

"So you're just going to pretend like nothing happened?"

"For now..."

"I knew it!" he exclaimed as he sat down... "Spill it!"

"I can't..."

"Did he threaten you?!"

"No – it's nothing like that..."

"So you're really not going to tell me?"

"Not yet..."

"Okay... I'll wait..." Smalls said as he got up to leave...

"Thank you Smalls..." she smiled as she hugged him...

"Easy – I'm married..." he laughed...

"And I'm divorced!" she sighed...

"Are you okay?"

"Yes..."

"Really?"

"I was upset yesterday – but now that it's over – I feel like a weight's been lifted off my shoulders..."

"It has..."

"I'll see you soon..."

"You will?" Smalls asked as he raised his eyebrow at her...

"Yea..." she sighed...

"Okay – see you soon..." he said as he left...

"Welcome to Cracker Barrel – what can I get for you this morning?" the waitress asked...

"We'll each have your Uncle Herschel's Favorite..." Sid answered...

"Hash brown casserole or fried apples?"

"One with the hash brown casserole – one with fried apples – we'll share..." Sid answered.

"Will that be ham, catfish, hamburger steak, chicken tenderloins, or pork chop?"

"Hhmmmmm... Amber... you pick..." Sid said.

"Catfish..." I answered.

"Very well – catfish it is – may I get some drinks for you?" the waitress asked.

"Coffee!" we both said.

"I'll be right back with your drinks..." the waitress said as she walked away...

"What happened in there?" I asked again...

"Well – after you left the court room – the judge granted the divorce and went over the settlement – and then he asked Jade if she was sure she only wanted $500k..."

"That's odd..."

"I thought so too..."

"Did Jade ask for more?"

"No..."

"Okay..."

"So then the judge wants to go over the petition for custody of the baby..."

"I thought that was already settled?'

"I thought so too – but when I said something, the judge told me not to speak until I was called to..."

"Where did that come from?"

"I have no idea..."

"I thought everything was pretty much finalized..."

"So did I..."

"What took you so long?"

"He told Smalls he needed to see Jade in his chambers – alone..."

"Really?"

"Yes..."

"Why?"

"I have no idea..."

"What did Smalls say?"

"He had no idea either..." Sid answered as the waitress put our coffee on the table...

"So you and Smalls waited while Jade was in the judge's chambers?"

"Yes..."

"I think Smalls knows what was going on..."

"I think we need to change the subject..."

"You do?"

"Yes..."

"What would you like to talk about then?"

"I'd like to talk about us getting married..."

"You just got divorced..."

"Exactly..."

"When do you want to get married?"

"I wish I could marry you today..."

"My wedding date will not be Friday, April 2nd, 2021..." I said as the waitress put our food on the table...

"Why not?"

"Are you serious right now?!" I snapped...

"Uh oh – this is about to go left – let's talk about something else – you asked me about the gemstones earlier – let's talk about that..."

"Okay..."

"I took the gemstones to Kay Jewelers..."

"Oh Sid!"

"I'm having wedding bands custom-designed for us with them..."

"I love you so much!" I exclaimed as I pulled him into a kiss...

"I love you too My Queen..."

"When did you do this?"

"Yesterday..."

"You really did have something to do..." I sighed...

"Yes I did..."

"When will they be ready?"

"About a week..."

"I can't wait to see them!"

"I wish we could set a date..." he sighed...

"We can set a date..."

"Good – as soon as we set a date we can give it to Winston..."

"Who's Winston?"

"Winston is the guy I spoke to at Kay Jewelers – he said we can have our rings engraved with the date before he gives them to us..." Sid explained as his phone rang...

"Gertrude?"

"Yes Jade..."

"I need to go to the infirmary..."

"Okay..." Gert sighed as she took Jade by the arm...

"Hello Jade..."

"Hi Donna..."

"Have you made a decision?"

"Yes..."

"What have you decided?"

"I'm going to have the abortion..."

"Are you sure? You don't need more time to think about it?"

"If I think about it any longer, I'll end up regretting it..."

"You may regret it anyway..."

"I've thought about it enough to know I'm doing what's best for me..." she sighed...

"Okay – have you decided which procedure you want?"

"I want the pill..."

"Okay – I'm going to schedule an appointment for you at Milford Hospital..."

"Why?"

"They'll be a lot of bleeding and cramping – you'll need a lot of maxi pads – and you'll need a heating pad – you'll need access to a health care professional for 24 hours..."

"Can't you be there for me?"

"You want to stay in the infirmary?"

"I want to stay with you..." she sighed...

"Let me explain the process..."

"Okay..."

"First, you take mifepristone – this stops the pregnancy from growing. You might feel nauseous or start bleeding after taking it. You'll also need to take antibiotics to prevent infection..."

"Okay..."

"The second medicine is misoprostol. You take this right away or up to 48 hours after you take the first one..."

"I don't want to wait 48 hours..."

"This medicine causes cramping and bleeding to empty your uterus. This will start 1 to 4 hours after taking the misoprostol. You'll see large blood clots or clumps of tissue – it's like having a really heavy, crampy period – or an early miscarriage..."

"Oh my God..."

"This can last for several hours..."

"Oh my God..."

"You'll be sent back here with a pregnancy test and then you'll have an ultrasound to make sure the abortion worked..."

"WHAT???!!!"

"Sometimes it doesn't work..." Donna sighed...

"Oh hell no – I'll have a regular abortion!"

"Okay – there are two types of regular abortions..."

"Two?"

"Yes – the first is suction – or vacuum aspiration – this is used if you're 16 weeks or less – the second one is D & E – dilation and evacuation – this procedure uses suction and medical tools to empty your uterus – this procedure is used when you're past 16 weeks..."

"Thank God I don't have to worry about that..."

"You don't have to spend the day in the hospital – but since you're an inmate – you have to go to the clinic..."

"Can you come with me?"

"I can be there if you want..."

"Thank you Donna..."

"You're welcome – I can get you an appointment right away..."

"That's fine with me..."

"Gert – she's ready..."

"Sid – can you come in to see me?" Winston asked...

"Sure – what's wrong?"

"I'll tell you when you get here..."

"Okay – we're on our way..."

"What's wrong?" I asked...

"Winston needs me to come see him..."

"Oh no – I hope everything's alright..." I sighed as we got up to leave...

Chapter 31

"Come with me..." Winston said as soon as he saw us...

"What's going on?" Sid asked...

"I'll show you..." Winston answered as we went into his office... "Wow!' he exclaimed as he watched the gemstones float up off the counter, start glowing, and circle us...

"They missed us..." I sighed...

"I've never seen anything like this!" Winston exclaimed... "No wonder they wouldn't sit right – they kept popping out the setting – I thought it was me!"

"I didn't think this would happen..." Sid laughed...

"They do this all the time?!"

"Yes..." I answered...

"My stones were in a fire – my fiancée saved them from being burned – we had them cleaned – and they've been glowing and spinning ever since..." Sid explained...

"Thank God you're here – maybe now I can do this for you..."

"We can stay here if you like..."

"Oh I'd like – I want to complete this for you – you two are special..."

"Yes we are..." Sid agreed as he went over to the rings, picked them up, and spoke to the stones... "This is what you were created for. Your sparkle and glow were meant to be seen. I've asked your mother, My Queen, to marry me – and she said yes – so I need you to let Winston set you so you can come back to us and be displayed the way you were destined to be..." Winston watched in amazement as the gemstones stopped circling us and settled back down on the counter...

"Thank God we have cameras in here – otherwise – no one would believe me!"

"Cameras?" I asked...

"Oh yes – we're under surveillance..."

"Is there any way you can delete that video?" Sid asked...

"I can talk to corporate..."

"Thanks – we don't want everybody to know about that..."

"I can understand that..." Winston acknowledged as he got to work. We watched as Winston began setting the stones, humming as he did so... "One done!" he exclaimed and then he went on to the next one. When he was finished, he brought both rings over for us to see...

"Oh Sid... they're beautiful!" I sighed...

"Yes they are..." Sid agreed...

"I'm glad you like them – I'll finish sealing them and then you can take them home – unless you've picked a wedding date..."

"Not yet..." Sid answered...

"Well you can pick a date now if you want..."

"Friday, May 7th, 2021..." I said...

"May 7th?" Sid asked...

"May 7th..." I repeated. Winston picked up a piece of paper, wrote something down on it, and showed it to us...

Obsidian & Amber Heart 5/7/21
Obsidian & Amber – Friday, May 7th, 2021
Obsidian & Amber – Friday, 5/07/21
Obsidian & Amber Heart – Friday, May 7th, 2021
Obsidian & Amber Heart – 5/07/21

"I like number 2..." Sid said...

"I like number 2 too..." I said...

""Okay – I'll finish setting these and then I'll have them engraved..."

"Thank you Winston..." Sid said...

"You're welcome – I'll call you when they're ready..."

"Well it's about time!" Chris exclaimed when she saw us...

"Chris! Chandra!" I exclaimed as I ran towards them and Maui ran towards me...

"Hi Maui!" I exclaimed as she jumped up on me... "Maui – this is Sid, My King..."

"Oh my God!" Chandra exclaimed as Maui bowed down...

"Up Maui..." Sid said. We all watched in amazement as Maui sat straight up...

"Oh wow – I've never, ever, seen Maui do that for anybody!" Chris exclaimed...

"I'm so happy to see you..." I sighed as we all hugged...

"May I cut in?" Sid asked as he put his arms around all of us...

"Oh – he's a hugger just like we are..." Chandra said...

"Hello Chandra, I'm Obsidian – my friends and family call me Sid...

"It's nice to meet you Sid – I've heard so much about you – I feel like I know you already..."

"C'mon – let's go upstairs..." Sid said as we walked into the building...

"Good evening Your Majesty..." Charles greeted... "Good evening Ladies – and good evening to you too..." he greeted as he pet Maui...

"Hi Charles – that's Maui – these are Maui's parents – Chris, and her wife, Chandra..."

"Do we have to leave Maui outside?" Chandra asked...

"Oh no – pets are allowed – and even if they weren't – Maui is welcome here anytime..." he said as he bent down to pet her again and she jumped up and kissed him in his mouth...

"Aww..." we all said...

"You're lucky I like you..." Charles laughed...

"C'mon Ladies – let's go upstairs..." Sid said. As soon as we got inside, the crystals and spheres came down the hall glowing and spinning...

"Oh my God! Hey!" Chris exclaimed...

"They look so beautiful!" Chandra exclaimed...

"Look at Maui!" Chris exclaimed as Maui was on her hind legs looking up at the crystals and spheres...

"Oh that's cute – I need to get a picture of that..." Chandra said...

"Get a video..." Chris suggested...

"Okay..." Chandra said as she took out her phone and just as she began recording, Maui stopped... "You tired Maui?"

"Maui's fascinated..." Sid said...

"Yes she is..." Chris agreed... "Do the crystals and spheres do this all the time?"

"Basically..." I laughed...

"They follow us everywhere we go..." Sid said...

"Everywhere?" Chandra asked...

"The first time we went to get in the shower, we closed the door – and I asked Sid what all the noise was – Sid opened the door and the crystals, gemstones, and spheres came in and started circling the ceiling!" I laughed...

"The crystals were knocking?! Aaah Haaa! Haah! Haah! Haah! Haah!" Chris laughed...

"That's crazy!" Chandra laughed...

"Wait a minute... where are the gemstones?" Chris asked...

"I took them to Kay Jewelers..." Sid answered...

"Ooohhh..." Chandra sighed...

"He dropped them off yesterday..." I added...

"Oh that's right – congratulations!" Chris exclaimed...

"Thank you..." we both said...

"Have you set a date?" Chandra asked...

"Friday, May 7th, 2021..." I answered...

"A month from now?" Chris asked...

"Sid wanted to get married today..." I laughed...

"Well damn – if you don't want us there Sid – just say so!" Chris laughed...

"It's not that... I promise..."

"You just can't wait to marry your Queen..." Chandra sighed...

"Yea..." Sid agreed...

"We went to court today..." I sighed...

"Oh boy – I don't need to ask how that went..." Chris said...

"Was it that bad?" Chandra asked...

"Well – the first thing she did was tell the judge she wanted me to leave the court room..." I laughed...

"Oh shit – what did the judge say?" Chris asked...

"By the time he asked Amber to leave the court, she was already out the door..." Sid laughed...

"Okay – you're laughing – that's a good sign..." Chris said...

"It's a great sign..." I sighed...

"Aww... that's beautiful..." Chandra said...

"I'm happy to move on..." Sid said...

"So am I..." I agreed...

"Well – it seems like the perfect time to celebrate..." Chris said as she pulled out a bottle of Dom Perignon from her bag..."

"Chris!" I exclaimed...

"I was waiting to make sure we were celebrating before I pulled this out..."

"Oh yes – we're definitely celebrating!" I exclaimed as Sid went to get champagne flutes out the kitchen cabinet...

Chapter 32

"This is Sid..."

"Mr. Heart – this is Winston from Kay Jewelers..."

"Hello Winston..."

"I spoke with corporate about your video..."

"Okay..."

"They have a proposition for you..."

"Really?"

"They want to run it as a commercial..."

"Oh wow..."

"When you come to pick up your rings, Mr. Guest would like to speak with you..."

"Mr. Guest?"

"Yes – he's from our corporate office..."

"What time will he be there?"

"What time can you be here?'

"I can be there at 1 p.m..."
"I'll let him know..."

"Who was that?' I asked...
"That was Winston..."
"Are the rings ready?"
"Yes... but..."
"But what?" I interrupted...
"Winston spoke to the corporate office...
"Ohh..."
"He said the corporate office wants to run our video as a commercial..."
"Wow!"
"So you're okay with that?"
"I'm okay with it if you are..."
"I'm not sure I'm okay with it..."
"What's wrong?'
"It wasn't supposed to be public – it was supposed to be between us..."
"Maybe it was supposed to be public..."
"What are you saying?"
"Everything that's happened so far has brought us together..."
"That's true – but that doesn't mean our private moment or our stones should be on display!"
"It doesn't mean they shouldn't be on display either..."
"I'm just not sure I want to do this..." Sid sighed...

"My King – the words you spoke were so commanding – like a leader – like a King – but they were also so romantic – so compassionate – so loving – what we have has survived past lives through time – and now we can celebrate that every time we see our commercial..."

"My Queen..." he breathed as he pulled me into a kiss... "I love you so much..."

"So you'll do it?"

"I'll do it..."

"What time do we need to be there?"

"1 p.m..."

"Mr. Guest – this is Mr. Obsidian Heart – and this is his fiancée, Amber..." Winston said as he introduced us...

"Please call me Gary..." he said as he shook Sid's hand and then mine..."

"Thank you Gary..."

"You're welcome – I'll get right to it – we saw your video and we want to feature you and your fiancée in a commercial..."

"How will that work?" Sid asked...

"We'll use the video from when you came in here, we'll add a few images of you and your fiancée wearing the rings, and we'll add music..."

"How long will the commercial air?"

"The commercial will air as long as it's popular..."

"Popular? I don't understand..."

"We get feedback on all our commercials from the public – we run their favorites – since you're getting married we can run your commercial every day – everyone loves romance..."

"So you'll run the commercial every day for how long?"

"Mr. Heart – we want to have an exclusive contract with you – this means every time we run your commercial – our commercial – you get paid $500 each time it airs..."

"Commercials air all day sometimes..." Sid acknowledged as he shook his head...

"Exactly..."

"Add my wife to the contract and you've got a deal..."

"Your wife?"

"Yes..."

"So you want us to wait until you're married to run the commercial?"

"Yes..."

"When are you getting married?"

"Friday, May 7th..."

"Hmmm – that's a month from now..."

"Is that a problem?"

"Well – we wanted to start running the commercial right away..."

"Sid..." I interrupted... "It's fine – let them run it..."

"My Queen – we do this together or we don't do it at all..."

"My King – we're already together..." I said as I took his hand...

"Okay – I'll do it – but I want the checks payable to Obsidian & Amber Heart..."

"Yes Sir Mr. Heart!" Gary exclaimed as he shook Sid's hand... "We'll send you a preview of the commercial before it airs – once you approve it – we're good to go!"

"Thank you Gary – I look forward to hearing from you..." Sid said as he got up from the table...

"I'll be back with your rings..." Winston said. We waited for Winston to come back with the rings and when he did, Sid's expression changed...

"What's wrong?" I asked...

"They look different..."

"Different how?"

"I don't know – something seems off..."

"Maybe you should try them on..." Winston suggested...

"My Queen..." Sid said as he put my ring on my finger...

"My King..." I said as I picked up his ring. Sid extended his hand and when I put the ring on his finger, the stones started glowing... "Sid... they're glowing!"

"That's better..." Sid sighed...

"I'm glad you're happy..." Winston sighed...

"Mr. Heart – I'm going to add that to the commercial – I'll get back to you..." Gary said as he hurried out the store...

"Winston?" Sid asked...

"Yes Mr. Heart?"

"Could you send me the surveillance before they turn it into a commercial?"

"Sure..."

"Thank you..."

"You're welcome..."

"Let's go see Beautiee..." Sid suggested...

"Okay..."

"Hey!" Bazil exclaimed when he saw us...

"Hey Bazil..." Sid said...

"Hey..." I said...

"What brings you here?"

"We need to see Beautiee..." Sid answered...

"Is everything alright?"

"Everything's fine..." I sighed...

"Come with me..." Bazil said. When we got to their office, Beautiee jumped up from behind her desk...

"Hey!" she exclaimed as she came to hug us...

"Hey..." we both responded...

"I'm so happy to see you – let's go to the conference room...

"Bazil – come with us!" Sid exclaimed...

"Okay..." When we got in the conference room, Beautiee started right in...

"So are you going to let me put Jade's pregnancy in the book?"

"No..." Sid answered...

"Okay... are you going to let me put Amber's pregnancy in the book?"

"No..."

"May I ask why?"

"No..."

"Did something happen to make you change your mind?"

"Nothing changed my mind – I never wanted it in there..."

"Okay... Are you going to.... you'll probably say no – but I'm gonna ask anyway..."

"What?'

"Are you going to let me put in the book that you slept with Jade?"

"I will allow you to put that in the book – but only if it's okay with Amber..."

"Oh my – I didn't expect that – Amber – what do you say?"

"I think you should put it in the book..."

"Really?"

"Beautiee – I started reading your autobiography – your husband cheated on you – you cheated on him – and you found your way back to each other. Sid went back to his wife – he got caught up in a moment – they were still married – I don't like it – but I get it..."

"Wow – you are something else..."

"So are you!" I laughed...

"Yes I am!" she laughed... "But I just caught something you said – you said they were still married – does that mean they're divorced?"

"Yes we are..." Sid confirmed...

"Are those wedding bands you're wearing?"

"Not yet..."

"Oh – so have you set a date?"

"Yes – but that's not for the book..."

"Okay..." Beautiee sighed...

"So - I wanted to come see you to let you know what happened at Kay Jewelers..."

"Is this going in the book?"

"Yes..."

"Okay! Tell me!" she exclaimed as she started the recorder...

"Bazil and I went to Kay Jewelers..."

"I'm going in the book too?" Bazil asked...

"Yes – anyway – we met with Winston and I picked out the rings. The next day, Winston calls me to tell me there's a problem with the stones..."

"Oh no..."

"He asked me to come in because each time he tried to set the stones, they fell out..."

"Oh wow..."

"So we go in his office and as soon as the stones see us, they float up off the counter and start glowing as they're circling around us..."

"What?!" Bazil and Beautiee exclaimed...

"Apparently the stones knew they weren't home so they wouldn't allow Winston to set them – until I spoke to them..."

"Oh my God!" Beautiee exclaimed...

"You actually spoke to the stones?" Bazil asked...

"Yes..."

"What did you say?" Beautiee asked...

"This is what you were created for. Your sparkle and glow were meant to be seen. I've asked your mother, My Queen, to marry me – and she said yes – so I need you to let Winston set you so you can come back to us and be displayed the way you were destined to be..."

"Oh my God – that's so beautiful..." Beautiee whispered as she started crying...

"Wow..." Bazil whispered...

"After I spoke to them, Winston tells us they have surveillance cameras in the store..."

"Oh my God! They have it on camera?" Beautiee exclaimed...

"Yes..."

"I wanna see!"

"You will..."

"I will?! Yes!!"

"Everybody will..."

"Everybody?"

"Gary Guest met with us from their corporate office – they're going to feature our video in a commercial – and every time it airs – we get paid..." Sid beamed...

"They could air that commercial every year on Valentine's Day, at Christmas – you basically have a lifetime contract..." Bazil said...

"I know..." Sid agreed...

"Thank you so much – my readers are going to love this!" Beautiee exclaimed...

"You're welcome – we need to get going..." Sid said as he got up..."

"It was good seeing you Sid..."

"Good seeing you too..."

"Nice to see you again Amber..." Beautiee said...

"Nice to see you too..."

When we got home, the crystals and spheres came rushing down the hall to greet us... "I'm calling Chris – she's not going to believe this..." I laughed...

"I'm going back to bed..." Sid said as he smiled at me mischievously...

"I'm coming..." I said as I followed him down the hall...

"Not yet – but you will be..." Sid said as he pulled me into his arms and helped me out of my clothes...

"Hey Amber!" Chris exclaimed...

"Are you sitting down?"

"Oh boy – hold on – le'me check on the food..." she answered as she went into the kitchen...

"Do you still have popcorn?"

"Oh shit – Chandra!"

"Yea Chris?"

"Dinner's gonna be late – I'm on facetime with Amber – she just asked me if I still have popcorn!"

"Hold on – don't start without me – I'll be right there – I'll pour the wine!" Chandra exclaimed as she came downstairs, went in the kitchen, and poured two glasses of wine as Chris put the popcorn in the microwave...

Chapter 33

"Ooh! Look how the gemstones are circling around them!!" Jade heard an inmate say...

"Oh my God!! Those rings are beautiful!!"

"Look how they're glowing!!"

"I love the way he spoke to them!!"

"What's going on?" Jade asked as she walked over to the other inmates...

"This is the new Kay commercial – look – they're running it again!!" the inmate squealed. Jade was numb as she watched. As tears began streaming down her face, the other inmates just thought she was emotional because it was romantic...

"You ladies need tissue?" Gert asked as she came over with a box of tissues...

"Thank you..." Jade said as she took a few tissues out of the box. The other inmates took tissues out the box as if they were entitled to them without saying anything...

"You're welcome!!" Gert snapped...

"Gertrude?"

"Yes Jade?"

"Could you take me to see Deputy Warden Hein?"

"Do you need to file a complaint?"

"No – I need to speak to Judge Dulberg..."

'I'on know about that – I think you should call your attorney..."

"I'm going to do that too..."

"Oh – okay – I wanna see this – c'mon!!" Gert exclaimed as she took Jade by the arm...

"Deputy Warden Hein?"

"Yes Gertrude?"

"I have an inmate that says she needs to speak to you..."

"Who is it?"

"Jade Heart..."

"Why does she need to speak with me? Why can't she speak to her attorney?"

"She said she needs to speak to you, Judge Dulberg, AND her attorney!"

"Really?! Okay – send her in..." Jade went into the warden's office and sat down...

"Thank you Deputy Warden Hein..."

"What's this all about?"

"Well – I need to speak to Judge Dulberg right away..."

"Why don't you just speak to your attorney?"

"Judge Dulberg asked me not to speak to my attorney until I give him an answer..."

"An answer? To what?"

"I can't tell you..."

"Okay – I'll get him on the phone for you..." he said as he dialed the judge...

"This is Judge Dulberg..."

"This is Deputy Warden Hein..."

"What can I do for you Deputy?"

"I'm sitting here with Jade Heart..."

"How's she doing?"

"Well – she says she needs to speak to you – I told her to call her attorney but she says you asked her not to call her attorney until she gives you an answer..."

"Put her on the phone..."

"You wanna talk to her?"

"I said put her on the phone..."

"Yes Sir..." he said and then he passed the phone to Jade...

"Hello?"

"Jade – how are you?"

"I'm here..."

"Do you have an answer for me?"

"Yes..."

"Yes? Did you just say yes?"

"Yes..."

"You've made me so happy..."

"When can I see you?"

"You can see me on our wedding day..."

"How long do I have to wait?"

"Can you wait until Friday?"

"This Friday?"

"Yes..."

"I can wait..."

"I'll call Smalls – he'll come see you before then – in the meantime I need to get my calendar cleared – give the phone back to the Deputy..."

"Okay – see you Friday..." Deputy Warden Hein looked at her strangely as she handed the phone back to him...

"Hello?"

"Deputy – please have Ms. Heart ready to leave on Friday – April 16th – to return on Monday, April 19th..."

"You're giving her a weekend pass?!"

"Yes..."

"I'll get right on it..."

"Thank you..." Judge Dulberg said and then he hung up...

"Gertrude – she's ready to go back to her cell..."

"C'mon Jade..." Gert said as she took Jade by the arm and they started down the hall... "Did you speak to the judge?"

"Yes..."

"You must know somebody – I've never had an inmate get the privileges you get..." she said as she took Jade back to her cell...

"This is Smalls..."

"Smalls – this is Dulberg..."

"What can I do for you Your Honor?"

"I need to see Jade back in court on Friday, April 16th – 9 a.m..."

"Is she being charged with another crime?"

"No..."

"Okay – I'll make sure she's there..."

"Thank you Smalls..."

"Jade Heart please report to the visiting area..." the warden said over the loud speaker...

"I wonder if it's Joel..." Jade said as she hurried over to the visiting area... "Smalls!"

"We need to talk..."

"I know..." she sighed as she smiled. When they got inside the attorney/client room, Smalls slammed the door... "What's wrong?! Are you mad at me?!"

"Not yet..." he laughed...

"What's that supposed to mean?!" Jade laughed...

"Why did I get a call from Judge Dulberg telling me to make sure you're back in court by Friday at 9 a.m.?"

"Because I'm getting married..."

"WHAT?!"

"When Joel wanted to see me in his chambers, he asked me to marry him..."

"Why didn't you tell me?!"

"Joel asked me to wait until I gave him an answer..."

"Congratulations!!" he exclaimed as he pulled Jade into a hug...

"Easy now – you're married!!" she laughed...

"Good ole Joel!!" he exclaimed...

"He's leaving the bench after we get married...

"Oh shit!"

"Don't say anything – I don't know if I was supposed to tell anybody that..."

"Okay – I'll keep it between us..."

"Will you give me away?"

"Really?"

"Yes..."

"I'd be honored to..."

"Thank you Smalls..."

"I'll see you Friday..."

"Sid!" I exclaimed as I shook him...

"Wha... what's wrong?" he asked sleepily...

"Our commercial's on!!" We both sat up in bed and turned up the television...

"At Kay Jewelers, we treat you like family. We'll design your rings to your specifications because we understand it's your day. We won't stop until we get it right..."

"My Queen..." Sid breathed as he kissed me...

"I could watch our commercial all day..." I sighed...

"Look..." Sid said as he pointed up towards the ceiling..."

"Do you think they watch us?"

"I'll let you know right now..." he breathed as he pulled me down on top of him, grabbed my ass, and pushed me down on his dick...

"Oh Sid..." I moaned...

"They're watching... Ugh..." he moaned as he pushed himself up inside me...

"Oh Sid!!" I moaned as I leaned back to look up at the ceiling and braced myself on his thighs...

"Yes... That's it... Ride it... Ugh..."

"Huh... Huh... Huh... Huh..."

"Ugh... Ugh... Ugh... Ugh..."

"Huh... Sid... I'm cumming..."

"CUM FOR YOUR KING!!" he growled...

"HAAH! HAAH! HAAH! HAAH! HHHAAAHHH!!"

"UGH! UGH! UGH! UGH! UUUGGGHHH!!"

"My King..." I panted as I collapsed on top of him...

"Yes My Queen..." he breathed...

"I'm a lil' dizzy..."

"I guess you can't watch them and ride my dick at the same time..."

"I may not be able to watch them while I'm riding your dick... but I bet I can watch them while I'm on my back..." I said as I took him by surprise and flipped him on top of me...

"Let's see about that..." he breathed as he spread my legs, eased himself inside me, and pushed his tongue in my mouth...

"CHRIS!! CHRIS!!"

"What's wrong?!" Chris asked as she hurried down the stairs and into the living room...

"The commercial – it's on!!"

"Oh wow – look at that!!" Chris exclaimed as they both started jumping up and down and Maui started barking...

"Mommy – look!!" Beautiee's daughter, Lydia exclaimed...

"Oh wow!! Go get Daddy!!" Beautiee exclaimed...

"I'll get him!!" Joy exclaimed...

"What's going on?!" Bazil asked as he came into the living room and saw the commercial...

"Oh wow – look at that!!" Bazil exclaimed...

"They're so pretty!!" Jay exclaimed...

"Daddy – did your rings do that when you married Mommy?" Joseph asked...

"No son..."

"Why not?" Jay asked...

"Mommy and Daddy got married in Las Vegas – Las Vegas didn't have any gemstones so we bought each other diamonds..."

"That's okay Mommy – Daddy can marry you again and then he can buy you a ring like that one!!" Lydia exclaimed...

"And Mommy can buy Daddy a ring like that one!!" Joseph exclaimed...

"I want a ring like that when I get married..." Joy said...

"Me too..." Jay said...

"By the time you get married – they'll have rings that are even more beautiful..." Beautiee sighed...

Chapter 34

"Amber... I need to talk to you..."

"Yes Sid?"

"Please don't be mad..."

"This is about Jade..." I sighed...

"Yes..."

"What is it Sid?"

"Well... I don't want to take the baby to see her in prison..."

"I don't want you to either..."

"Judge Dulberg already told me he'd grant her visitation..."

"Maybe she'll change her mind..."

"Do you mind if I go talk to her?"

"I don't mind..."

"Really?"

"Either she'll say yes or no..." I sighed...

"Thank you..." he breathed as he pulled me into a kiss...

"For what?"

"For loving me..."

"Jade Heart please report to the visiting area..." the warden said over the loud speaker...

"Hmmm – I wonder who it is now?" she said as she went to the visiting area... "What the hell are you doing here?!" she snapped...

"Oh my God – look!! It's him!!" one of the inmates exclaimed...

"Who?!"

"The guy from the commercial!!" she screamed as she hurried over to Sid... "Excuse me – may I have your autograph?"

"I want a picture!!"

"Me too!!"

"Oh my God!! That ring!!"

"Jade – why didn't you tell us you knew this guy?!"

"What the hell is going on here – oh my God – it's you!!" Gert exclaimed...

"Yes – it's me..." Sid sighed as he smiled...

"Sorry – but I want a picture too..." she said as she took out her phone...

"I'll tell you what – le'me speak to Jade in private – and then I'll let you all take pictures with me..."

"C'mon – I'll show you the attorney/client room..." Gert said as Sid got up...

"Damn Jade – he is fine – I wish he was coming to see me!!" one of the inmates yelled as they went down the hall...

"Okay Sid – why are you here?!"

"I was hoping you'd reconsider visitation..."

"Excuse me?!"

"I was hoping you'd let us raise the baby and you'd wait until you got out of prison to petition for visitation..."

"You selfish, pompous, arrogant ass!!" Jade laughed...

"What's so funny?!"

"You – and your Queen!!" she laughed...

"What about us?!"

"I've seen the commercial – you think you're just going to ride off into the sunset and live happily ever after with my child!!" she laughed...

"You can be a part of his life – I just don't think..."

"Sid..." she laughed... "Stop... I can't!!"

"Why are you laughing?!"

"You never loved me – and you don't love her either – but that's none of my business – you're her problem now – not mine!!" she laughed...

"We just want what's best for the kids!!"

"Kids?! She's pregnant?!"

"Yes..."

"You mother fucker!! Did you even let the ink dry on our divorce papers – oh wait – never mind – she was pregnant before we got divorced – thank God I had an abortion..."

"WHAT??!! YOU HAD AN ABORTION??!!"

"Yes!! I had an abortion!!"

"WHY??!!"

"I had an abortion so I wouldn't have to explain to my child that I tried to kill his other Mommy!!"

"I can't believe you killed my son!! How could you?!"

"Same way you killed us Sid..." she sighed...

"You're a MONSTER!! What did I ever see in you?!"

"Apparently you never saw anybody but yourself..."

"Good bye Jade..."

"Good bye – and good riddance!" Jade snapped as Sid slammed the door...

"You're leaving?!" Gert asked...

"Oh yes – pictures – I almost forgot..."

"C'mon..." Gert said as he followed her back to the visiting area...

"There he is!!" one of the inmates squealed as they started running towards him...

"Uh uh – I'll shit this shit down – y'all better back the fuck up!!" Gert snapped...

"Ladies – I'm happy to take a few pictures with you..." Sid said as they calmed down and began to line up...

"Hey..." I sighed as Sid came in...

"Hey..."

"Oh my God – what happened?!" I asked as Sid broke down... "Come here..." I took Sid's hand, led him to the couch, and let him cry on my shoulder as the crystals and spheres glowed and circled in the ceiling above us...

"She killed my son..." he sobbed...

"Oh Sid... I'm sorry..."

"Please don't kill my daughter..."

"Never..."

"She was so cruel..."

"I'm sorry..."

"I told her I wanted her to reconsider visitation..."

"She didn't want to?"

"She called me a selfish, arrogant, pompous ass – and then she laughed..."

"What a Bitch!"

"She asked me if I just thought we were going to ride off into the sunset and live happily ever after with her child..."

"We just wanted what was best for the baby!"

"I tried to tell her we wanted what was best for the kids – she asked me if I let the ink dry on our divorce papers before you got pregnant – and then..."

"What Sid?"

"She said I never loved her – and I don't love you either – I only love myself..."

"My King – I know you love me... and I know you loved her too..."

"I did – but after what she said when I asked her why she had an abortion – I don't think I ever knew her at all..."

"What did she say?"

"She said she had an abortion so she wouldn't have to explain to him that she tried to kill his other Mommy..." he cried...

"Oh Sid... I'm sorry..."

"How could she be so cruel?"

"It's easy to be cruel when you've lost everything..." I sighed...

"Sid..."

"Mom?!"

"Hi Daddy..."

"You don't have to worry about him – I've got him..."

"I'm okay Daddy – I'm with Grandma..."

"I love you Obi..."

"I love you too Daddy..."

"Obi – I like that..." his mother said as she rocked him..."

"I wish you could meet Amber..."

"We'll see you soon – take care of my granddaughter..."

"I will Mom... I promise..." I cried with him as he cried in his sleep...

Chapter 35

"Good morning..." I yawned...

"Good morning..." he sighed...

"Where do you want to get married?"

"Let's get married at the Taylor Inn Bed & Breakfast in Boston..."

"Okay..."

"Okay?! Just like that?!"

"Yes..."

"You're not going to ask me about the place or anything?!"

"I'll find out everything I need to know when I go plan our wedding..." I sighed...

"I love you..."

"I love you too..."

"I have something to tell you..."

"Okay..."

"Yesterday – when I went to see Jade..."

"We don't need to talk about that anymore..." I interrupted...

"Oh so you don't care that I had women all over me?!"

"What are you talking about?!" I exclaimed as I sat up...

"They recognized me from the commercial!!" he laughed...

"So you're a celebrity..."

"Yes..."

"How did it feel?"

"I'll be honest – I liked it – they all wanted to take pictures with me – some of them even wanted my autograph..."

"I'm glad you don't have to go back there..."

"So am I..."

"Let's go get our marriage license..."

"Okay..."

"I need to ask you something..."

"Yes My Queen?"

"When are we going back to work?"

"As soon as you re-decorate – I can't go in there right now..."

"Okay – I need to ask you something else..."

"Okay..."

"How many children do you want?"

"I never thought about it..."

"Does that mean I'm having another baby?"

"Yes..."

"Okay – that means we need a bigger place..."

"Yes it does..."

"Between planning our wedding, redecorating, and house hunting – I'm going to be very busy!"

"What would you like to do first?"

"I want to go get our marriage license..."

"Okay..."

"Congratulations Judge Dulberg..." the clerk said...

"Not for long..." he laughed...

"You're retiring?!"

"I'm retiring..."

"Congratulations!!"

"Thank you..."

"I guess you're going to enjoy your retirement with your new bride..."

"Yes I am..." he answered as he pulled Jade into a kiss...

"So this is why you got an abortion..." Sid said as we walked in...

"Mr. Heart..." the judge started to say...

"Congratulations to you both..." Sid interrupted as he shook his head...

"Thank you..." Jade said...

"C'mon Jade – let's go get married..." he said as he put his arm around her...

"Okay Joel..." she sighed as they walked out...

"Do you know them?" the clerk asked...

"I have no idea who they are..." Sid sighed...

"Okkaayyy... how may I help you today?"

"We're here to get our marriage license..." Sid answered as I smiled...

"Aww... congratulations..."

"Thank you..." we both said...

"Do you have valid identification?"

"Yes we do..." Sid answered as he pulled out his license and I pulled out mine...

"I need to make a copy of these to attach to your application – I'll be right back..." she said as she walked over to the copy machine. Sid and I looked at each other and smiled...

"Here ya go..." she said as she gave us back our licenses...

"I need you both to fill this out completely – once you fill it out – I'll look it over, make sure it's filled out properly, and then we'll all sign it..."

"Okay..." Sid said as he took the form. I watched anxiously as he filled out his side – I wanted him to hurry up so I could fill out mine...

"Here, here!" He laughed as he gave it to me. I studied his side and read his parent's information: Mother – Phyllis Heart, Father – June Heart. I started filling out my side with my name, date of birth, social security number, etc., and then I filled in my parent's information: Mother – Connie Morrison, Father – Jake Morrison. I went down the rest of the form and compared my answers to Sid's: City of Birth – Bridgeport, State – CT, Prior Marriages – Yes/No, Maiden Name – Amber Morrison, Name on Marriage Certificate – I got another piece of paper and wrote two names: Amber Morrison Heart, Amber Heart...

"I like this one..." I said out loud as I wrote Amber Heart on the form. After I filled in the name to be put on the Marriage Certificate I saw Sid's signature at the bottom of the form and I started crying after I signed my name...

"Aww..." the clerk said as she handed me tissues...

"Sorry..." I laughed...

"Don't ever apologize for happiness..." she said as she took the form and read it over...

"Obsidian?" she asked...

"Yes?"

"Did you fill this out of your own free will?"

"Yes Maam..."

"Is this your signature?" she asked as she pointed to his signature...

"Yes Maam..."

"Amber?"

"Yes?"

"Did you fill this out of your own free will?"

"Yes Maam!"

"Is this your signature?" she asked as she pointed to my signature…

"Yes Maam!"

"Okay…" she said as she signed the form. "I'm going to process this and get you your license – once I do that – you can get married anytime you want – but you have to get married within 60 days – if you don't get married in 60 days, it will expire – and you'll be back to see me… I'll be right back…" she said as she went into the office behind the counter…

"I love you My King…"

"I love you too My Queen…" Sid said and then he kissed me…

"Here's your license…" the clerk said as she handed us our license. We looked at the license, and then we looked at each other…

"Do you have any questions?" I looked at our license again and read the signature at the bottom:

Prepared by: Alberta Woody
Title: City Clerk
City: Bridgeport
State: CT

"No…" I sighed…

"Do you have any questions Obsidian?"

"No Maam…"

"On your wedding day – give this license to the wedding officiant – they'll sign it, date it, and then they'll mail it out to Vital Records for the state you get married in and a copy of it will also be sent here. You'll receive your Marriage Certificate from the Vital Records Office…"

"Thank you Ms. Woody…" I said as I gave her a hug…"

"You can call me Alberta…" she said as she pulled us both into a hug and started crying…

"You okay?" Sid asked…

"I'm fine – I'm just happy…" she said as she wiped her eyes…"

"Aww… we're happy too… " Sid said as we all hugged…

"Is it true?"

"Yes Joel…" Jade sighed…

"Why didn't you tell me?"

"Because I wanted today to be about us…"

"Look in the closet…" Jade looked in the closet and she started crying when she saw her dress and a pair of shoes…

"Joel… Thank you…"

"I want you to get dressed – and then we're going to Judge Duffey's court room – and we're going to be married…"

"Yes Your Honor…" she sniffed as she took the dress out the closet and went into the bathroom…

"Congratulations Joel…" the judge said…

"Thank you – Jade – this is Judge Harland Duffey – Harland – this is my bride to be, Jade..."

"It's nice to meet you – congratulations..." Judge Duffey said as he took Jade's hand and kissed it...

"Thank you – I still can't believe it..."

"We've been friends a long time – It's an honor to perform the ceremony for you both..."

"Thank you..." Jade sighed...

"Nice to see you again Smalls..." Judge Duffey said as he walked in with his wife...

"Smalls..." Jade whispered when she saw him...

"Jade, this is my wife, Josefina..."

"It's so nice to meet you – you're very beautiful..." Jade said...

"Thank you – you're very beautiful too..." Josefina said as they hugged each other...

"Shall we get started?" Judge Duffey asked...

"Absolutely..." Judge Dulberg answered...

"Beloved... we are gathered here this afternoon to join my dear friend and colleague, Joel Dulberg, and Jade Heart in marriage. You have both come before me, expressed your desire to become husband and wife. Do you have rings?"

"Yes – we have rings..." Judge Dulberg answered said as he took two ring boxes out his pocket...

"I don't have a ring for you..." Jade whispered...

"Just put this ring on my finger..." Judge Dulberg said...

"Okay – take the rings out the boxes – Jade – you take his ring – Joel – you take her ring..."

"Okay..." they both said...

"Who gives this woman to be married? Judge Duffey asked...

"I do..." Smalls answered...

"Okay – Joel – do you have anything you want to say to Jade?"

"Yes I do..." He answered as he took Jade's hands...

"Jade, when you first came into my court, I didn't know what to expect. It was just a regular work day for me until you spoke. Something came over me – a feeling that I haven't felt in a long time. Thank you for giving me another chance to love again..."

"Okay – Jade – do you have anything you want to say to Joel?"

"Yes I do..." She answered as she took Joel's hands...

"Joel – when you wanted to see me in your chambers I had no idea what to expect. I couldn't understand how you developed feelings for me – but thank God you did. Thank you for loving me in spite of me. I'm going to spend the rest of our lives making you as happy as you're making me right now......" Joel started crying and took Jade's face in his hands and kissed her...

"Joel – put the ring on Jade's finger and repeat after me..." Judge Duffey said...
"Okay – I'm ready..." he said...

"Jade – I take you as my wife, with your faults and your strengths, as I offer myself to you with my faults and my strengths..." Joel repeated after Judge Duffey and then he continued... "I will help you when you need help and turn to you when I need help. Today - I choose to spend the rest of my life with you..." Jade started crying as Joel took her face in his hands and kissed her...

"Jade – put the ring on Joel's finger and repeat after me..."
"Okay – I'm ready..." she said...

"Joel - I take you as my husband, with your faults and your strengths, as I offer myself to you with my faults and my strengths. I will help you when you need help and turn to you when I need help. Today – I choose to spend the rest of my life with you..." Joel cried as Jade repeated the vows to him. When she was finished, he took her face in his hands and kissed her again...

"Joel, Jade, you have come before God, your friends, and me to pledge your love and commitment to each other. By the power invested in me by God and to me by the State of Connecticut, I now pronounce you Mr. & Mrs. Joel Dulberg!!" They were both kissing profusely before Judge Duffey could tell Joel to kiss his bride...

"Okay – I need everyone to get together for pictures!" Judge Duffey announced... "Bailiff?"
"Yes Your Honor?"
"Would you do the honors?"
"Absolutely!!" he exclaimed...
"Okay – let's make this easy for him – everybody put your phones on the table – we'll pose – he'll take the pictures – we'll all have them in our phones..." Judge Duffey suggested. When they were done taking pictures, Joel stopped Smalls as he was about to leave... "Smalls – I need to speak to you in private..."
"Yes Your Honor..." Smalls said as he followed him into Judge Duffey's chambers... "I have a surprise for my wife – and I'd like you and your wife to come with us..."
"Okay – that's fine..."

"Good – let's go!" he exclaimed as they went back into the court room...

"Where are we going?" Jade asked...

"You'll see..." he answered...

Chapter 36

"**Congratulations** Mr. & Mrs. Dulberg – right this way..." the hostess said as they followed her to their table...

"Good afternoon..." the waitress greeted... "Welcome to Village Bistro. Congratulations on your wedding..."

"Thank you..." they both said...

"May I start you all off with our featured drink, Lousi M. Mautini Caberenet Sauvignon, or would you like something else?"

"We'll have two bottles of Dom Perignon..." Joel answered...

"Yes Sir – I'll be right back..." she said as she went to get the Champagne...

"Everyone please raise you glass..." Joel said as he stood up and went to the front of the table... "Jade, please stand beside me..." Jade went to stand beside him and then he continued... "Here's to all of us..."

"To all of us..." they all said in unison as they sipped their champagne...

"How's everything here?" the waitress asked as she came back to the table...

"We'll have Fried Calamari, Crab Cakes, Hot Shot Buffalo Wings, Fried Brussel Sprouts, and Mussels Scampi..." Joel said...

"Fried Calamari, Crab Cakes, Hot Shot Buffalo Wings, Fried Brussel Sprouts, and Mussels Scampi – got it!" she said as she went to get our appetizers...

"I'ma have the Seafood Risotto..." Smalls said

"I'll have the Cajun Grilled Atlantic Cod..." Josefina said...

"I'll have the Chicken Francaise..." Jade said...

"I'm going to have the Grilled Center Cut Filet Mignon..." Joel said as the waitress came back over to the table...

"Looks like you've decided..." the waitress said...

"We have..." Joel said...

"Okay – I'm ready..."

"Grilled Center Cut Filet Mignon, Chicken Francaise, Seafood Risotto, and Cajun Grilled Atlantic Cod ‐ And two more bottles of champagne..." Joel said...

"Good thing we don't have to drive..." Jade laughed...

"I don't have to work tomorrow – I mean not in the court room..." Joel laughed as Jade pulled him into a kiss...

"Aww..." Smalls and Josefina said as the waitress and waiter brought their appetizers to the table...

"Damn this looks good – and I'm hungry!" Jade exclaimed..."

"Si, si..." Josefina said as they all started passing the plates and helping themselves...

"More champagne?" the waitress asked...

"Yes please!" Joel said...

"None for me..." Smalls said...

"No thank you..." Josefina said...

"Yes, thank you..." Jade said...

"How was the food?" the waitress asked...

"I hate Brussel sprouts – but now that I've tasted yours – I like them..." Jade said...

"I'll be sure to pass that on..." the waitress said... "How was everything else?"

"Good!" they all answered...

"That's great – we'll be back with your food in a lil' bit..." she said as she walked away...

"Ooohhh... this all looks so good..." Jade said...

"Who has the Seafood Risotto?"

"Me..." Smalls said...

"Who has the Cajun Grilled Atlantic Cod?"

"Ci, ci..." Josefina said...

"Who has the Grilled Center Cut Filet Mignon?"

"Right here..." Joel said...

"Who has the Chicken Francaise?"

"That's for me! Jade exclaimed..."

"Alright! I know you just got your dinner but please feel free to let me know if you want dessert – today our dessert is Double Fudge Chocolate Cake..." she said as she walked away...

"Ooohhh.... This looks so good!" Joel said...

"Damn this shit is good!" Smalls said...

"Shall I bring the cake?" the waitress asked...

"Yes please..." Joel answered. The waitress brought the cake to the table and Joel started cutting the cake, and passed down the plates...

"Mmmm... this is good..." Jade sighed...

"It sure is!" Josefina agreed. They all ate, laughed, and talked until they couldn't eat anymore and Joel began to stretch...

"I'm ready..."

"We're ready too..." Smalls said...

"Thank you for coming..." Joel said

"You're welcome..."

"Thank you for a lovely afternoon – it was lovely meeting you all..." Josefina said...

"Okay Mrs. Dulberg – let's go home..." Joel said as they all got up to leave...

"Home... I never thought I'd hear that word again..."

"You'll hear it often..." Joel said as he pulled her into a kiss... "I'll see you all outside..." Joel said as he went to pay the check. When they got outside, Smalls and Josefina were waiting to give them hugs and kisses...

"Congratulations..." Smalls said...

"Thank you Smalls..." Joel said...

"Congratulations..." Josefina said as she hugged Jade..."

"Thank you..." Jade said. Joel waited for them to leave before he whispered in Jade's ear...

"Are you ready for your wedding night Mrs. Dulberg?"

"Yes Mr. Dulberg – I'm ready..."

"I can't wait to get you home..." he said as he took her hand and led her to the limo...

"This is home..." Jade sighed as they pulled up in front of the house...

"Yes... this is home... I hope you like it..." Joel said as he opened the door for her and she got out...

"I love it!" she squealed as she threw her arms around him...

"Welcome home..." he said as he picked her up in his arms and carried her up the stairs leading to the front porch... "Take the keys out my top pocket..." Jade took the keys out his pocket... "Open the door..." Jade opened the door and Joel carried her into the house and put her down... "Come with me..." he said as he took her hand and led her into his library... "Sit down... we need to talk..."

"Okay..."

"I applied to have your sentence changed to an Intermittent Sentence..."

"What does that mean?"

"That means you serve your time Monday through Friday – but you come home on weekends..."

"Can you do that?!"

"Absolutely – we do that for inmates all the time – normally the inmates work Monday through Friday and only serve weekends – but in your case – it's reversed..."

"But I got 12 years – how does this work for me?

"In your case – you'll have to add 3 days a week onto your sentence – that's 3 days a week times 52 weeks – that's an additional 156 days a year times 12 years – you'll serve an extra 1,872 days in jail..."

"So I get more time?"

"You're still doing 12 years in prison – but because you're getting out on the weekends it will take longer for you to complete 12 years..."

"It sounds like I'm doing 5 more years in jail..."

"You are – but you're free on weekends..."

"I can't believe you did this for me..."

"I couldn't let you spend our wedding night in jail..."

"I thought I was going to get married in my jumpsuit and be back in my cell tonight..."

"Would you like to see the rest of our home?" he asked as he got up and extended his hand...

"Yes..." Joel took her hand, helped her up, and began showing her around...

"This is the living room..."

"Okay..."

"This is the dining room..."

"Okay..."

"This is the kitchen..."

"Oohhh... I can see myself making coffee and sitting on the back porch..."

"C'mon – I'll show you the bedrooms..." he said as he took her hand and led her upstairs... "There are three bedrooms and two bathrooms up here – there's a full bath off the library downstairs too..."

"This is huge!" Jade exclaimed...

"This is the 1st bedroom..."

"I like this one..."

"This is the bathroom..."

"It's big – two sinks, nice shower..."

"This bathroom connects to the second bedroom..."

"Oh – Jack & Jill..." she said as she looked in the 2nd bedroom...

"This is our bedroom..." he said as he took her inside...

"Oh my God! This is beautiful!" The master suite looked like a bedroom from an estate. The king-size bed was huge and Joel had rose petals all over it...

"Joel..." she whispered. There was a bucket of champagne on ice on the table by the chaise lounge, and the panoramic view out the bedroom window covered the Long Island Sound. Joel took Jade in his arms and kissed her sensually... "Make love to me..." she breathed...

"Are you sure?"

"Yes..." Joel slid her dress down off her shoulders and when it fell to the floor, he smiled...

"You're not wearing anything but your shoes..."

"I know..." she said as he picked her up in his arms, carried her to the bed, and laid her down gently. Jade watched him intently as he undressed and when he dropped his pants and boxers, she gasped at the size of his dick...

"I'll be gentle..." he whispered as he climbed up on the bed, spread her legs, and to her surprise, he began kissing her down her body...

"Joel... I..."

"Ssshhh..." he whispered as he continued kissing down her stomach. When he reached her pussy, her legs began to tremble as he spread her lips with his hands... "Hello Beautiful..." he breathed before he dove in...

"Jooeelll!!" she moaned as she arched her back and gripped the covers. Joel was gentle - but his tongue was relentless as he swirled around her clit and inside her pussy... "Haah... Haah... Haah..." Jade rode his face and each time she rose up off the bed his tongue went in deeper...

"Mmmm...." he moaned as she settled back down on the bed and he applied more pressure to her clit...

"Joel... Fuck... I'm cumming! I'm cumming!" she cried out as she grabbed his head and rode his face. Joel continued devouring her until she rode out her orgasm and when she relaxed her grip around his head he came up between her legs, lifted her right leg up, and eased himself inside her... "Oh God... Yes..." she moaned as he began thrusting...

"Yeesss..." he growled in her ear as he pushed himself in deeper...

"Joel... Huh... Fuck... Don't stop..." she moaned as she pulled him down on top of her. Joel increased his tempo and began fucking her harder... "Haah... Haah... Haah... Haah..."

"Fuck... Cum with me!" he growled...

"HAAH! HAAH! HAAH! HAAH! HAAH!"

"UGGH! UGGH! UGGH! UGGH! UGGH!"

"Oh Joel..." she panted as he flipped her on top of him...

"Sit up!!" he commanded...

"Ooohhh..." she moaned when she realized he was still hard...

"Ride my dick!!" he commanded as he grabbed her hips...

"Joel! Haah! Yes!"

"Fuucckkk!!" he growled as he thrust himself up inside her...

"Oh God! Joel! Fuck me!" she cried out a she threw her head back and her legs trembled around him...

"Yes! Ride my dick! Just like that! Fuck!"

"HAAH! HAAH! HAAH! HAAH! HAAH!"

"UGGH! UGGH! UGGH! UGGH! UGGH!"

"Oh my God!" she panted as she collapsed on top of him..."

"Not God..." he breathed as he pulled her into a kiss... "Just me..."

"Yes..." she breathed as she began kissing him down his chest...

"Jade..." he breathed as he played in her hair. Jade ignored him as she kissed him down his stomach... "Jade... you don't have to..."

"I want it..." she breathed and then she took him in her mouth...

"Fuucckkk!!" he moaned as she took him in all the way down to his balls. It took a minute for her to adjust to his length and girth as she gagged but she was determined...

"You okay?" he whispered as he moved her hair out the way so he could look at her...

"Mmm Hmm..." she moaned as she grabbed his hips and began sucking his dick...

"Uggh!!" he growled as he thrust his dick up in her mouth. Jade was gagging but she didn't stop – she relaxed her throat and her jaws, let the saliva run down on his balls, and continued... "Jaadddeee... Fffuuuuccckkk!!" he growled as he came in her mouth. Jade swallowed every drop and continued sucking until he stopped trembling...

"Oh my God..." he panted...

"Not God..." she panted as she came up between his legs and lay down on his chest... "Just me..."

"I have a confession..."

"Yes Joel?"

"That was my first time..."

"Stop it..." she laughed...

"I'm serious..."

"Oh wow..."

"You're the only one that wasn't afraid..."

"I have a confession to make too..."

"Tell me..."

"I was afraid..."

"You were? Why?"

"I didn't want to disappoint you..."

"You could never disappoint me..." he breathed as he pulled her into a kiss...

Chapter 37

"Thank you for calling Taylor House Bed & Breakfast – this is Darryl..."

"Hello Darryl – this is Amber Morrison..."

"Hello Ms. Morrison – how may I help you?"

"I'm getting married on Friday, May 7th..."

"Congratulations!"

"Thank you..."

"Would you like to have the ceremony here?"

"Yes..."

"Okay – we normally require a minimum of 10 people for the reception..."

"I think it'll be 11 - 10 people and a dog..."

"Did you say a dog?"

"I'm inviting my best friend and her wife to the wedding – they may want to bring their dog..."

"We don't allow dogs in the dining room – but if the dog's going to be in the wedding..."

"Yes – Maui's going to be in the wedding!" I interrupted..."

"Okay – on our website I want you to go to the estimate page..."

"Okay..." I said. I started filling out everything on the page from the guest count, event day, season, cocktail hour, menu type, beverage package, and all the services... "I'm so happy you can do all this..."

"No problem at all Ms. Morrison – we have four rooms available on May 7th for overnight – I'll describe each room..."

"I'll take all four..." I said...

"Okay – great – now do you see the estimate below at the bottom?"

"Yes I do..."

"I need to tell you that it's just an estimate – pricing could go up or down depending on whether you upgrade and it's subject to change..."

"That's fine – I'll take it – if it goes up – we'll make the adjustments – if it goes down – you'll make the adjustments..." I laughed...

"Okay – will that be cash, check, or charge?"

"It'll be charge - here's my card number..."

"You're all set – the time, instructions, check-inn, etc., will be forwarded to you – just call if you have any questions – what's your email?"

AmberMorrison@yahoo.com - and please send an email to ChrisMaron@gmail.com - I'll spell that for you... Darryl listened as I spelled out everything...

"Okay Ms. Morrison – you're all set – you'll hear from us shortly – do you have any questions?"

"Yes – will Maui be allowed to stay overnight in the room?"

"Yes – they'll be an extra charge to cover damages – but that'll be refunded to your credit card as long as there aren't any damages..."

"Thank you Darryl – I'll have Chris call you..."

"You're welcome – have a great day..."

"Hey!!" Chris exclaimed...

"Hey..." I sighed...

"We saw the commercial – oh my God!! We were jumping up and down and screaming – Maui was barking – we love it!!"

"Thanks..." I sighed...

"Okay – what's wrong?"

"Sid went to see Jade yesterday..."

"Oh boy..."

"He wanted to convince her to reconsider visitation..."

"Oh boy..."

"She was so cruel..."

"That doesn't surprise me..."

"She told him she had an abortion because she didn't want to explain to her son that she was in jail for trying to kill his other Mommy..."

"Oh my God..."

"He broke down and begged me not to kill his daughter..." I said as I started crying...

"Oh Amber..."

"His mother came to visit him last night – she was holding his son..."

"Oh my God – you saw that?"

"I heard it..."

"You heard it?"

"He called his mother... he said I love you Obi... and he said I wish you could meet Amber..."

"Oh wow..."

"He cried in his sleep and I cried with him..."

"Did you ask him about it?"

"I asked him where he wanted to go get married..."

"So where are you getting married?"

"Taylor Inn Bed & Breakfast in Boston..."

"Nice..."

"I told him I wanted to go get our marriage license..."

"That was a good idea..."

"I asked him how many children he wanted..."

"Oh wow – what'd he say?"

"He said he hadn't thought about it so I asked him if that meant I was having another baby and he said yes..."

"Ooohhh..."

"I told him we need a bigger place..."

"I bet he liked the sound of all that..."

"He did – he was happy until we went to get our marriage license..."

"What happened?!"

"We walked in on Jade and Judge Dulberg getting their marriage license..." I sighed...

"WHAT??!!"

"As soon as Sid saw her, he says so this is why you got the abortion..."

"Oh shit!"

"So then the judge puts his arm around Jade and says c'mon – let's go get married..."

"WHAT??!!"

"So then the clerk asks if he knows them and Sid says he has no idea who they are..."

"He'll never forgive her for that..."

"I know..."

"If she didn't want his baby – she could've just let you adopt..."

"She wanted to hurt Sid..."

"So did you get your marriage license?"

"Yes..."

"Thank God..."

"That's why I called you..."

"What do you need?"

"I need you to help me plan our wedding..."

"I'd love too..."

"Good because I already booked it and I told him you'll be calling him – he sent you an email..."

"Are dogs allowed?"

"He said dogs aren't allowed in the dining room but I told him Maui was going to be in the wedding and Maui can stay in the room with you – they just charge extra for damages..."

"Maui's a good girl – she won't damage the property..."

"I know..."

"Okay – I'll get right on this..."

"Thanks Chris..."

"You're welcome..."

"Was that Amber?" Chandra asked...

"Yea..."

"How's everything?"

"Fine – finally..."

"What now?"

"Well – Jade isn't pregnant anymore..."

"Really?!"

"Sid went to see her to ask her to reconsider visitation – she told him she had an abortion because she didn't want to explain to her son that she's in jail for trying to kill his other Mommy!"

"Oh that just cruel..."

"Amber said he broke down and begged her not to kill his daughter..."

"Oh my God..."

"I know – so they went to City Hall to get their marriage license – and they ran into Jade and Judge Dulberg..."

"Oh my God!"

"I know – right?"

"How'd she pull him?"

"Maybe she pulled him..." Chris answered as she mimicked the sucking motion with her mouth and her hand...

"Oh my God – you're so bad!" Chandra laughed...

"That's not what you said last night..." Chris laughed...

"Did you really just go there?!" Chandra laughed...

"I sure did!" Chris laughed...

"So do they have a venue?"

"Taylor Bed & Breakfast in Boston..."

"Oh that's a beautiful location..."

"Good – 'cause she put me in charge of helping her plan it!" Chris exclaimed...

"We're going?!"

"Absolutely!!"

"Oh Chris..." Chandra sighed as she pulled her into a kiss...

"I love you too..."

"I wonder if Maui can go..."

"Of course she can – Amber told Darryl Maui was in the wedding – we'll just buy her a little dress and tell them Maui's the flower girl..." Chris answered as she kissed Chandra again...

Chapter 38

"Thank you for calling Uneebo – this is Ashley..."

"Hi Ashley – my name is Amber – I'm calling on behalf of Heart Tech..."

"Heart Tech? I've heard of them – how can I help you?"

"We had a fire at the main office in Bridgeport..."

"Oh I'm sorry to hear that..."

"Thank you – since we have to reconstruct a bit, I thought it would be a good time to give the office a facelift – and if my husband likes it – we'll give his other locations a facelift as well..."

"Oh that's great! Have you checked out our website?"

"I'm on it now – and I like what I see..."

"That's nice to hear — have you taken our style quiz?"

"Not yet — I want to get my husband's input..."

"Okay Amber — as soon as you fill out the style quiz, I'll get back to you within 24 hours..."

"How long will this take?"

"The process normally takes between 6 to 8 weeks, depending on what you want — but the good thing is you don't have to go shopping for other services — we have packages that include a consultation, furniture, mood boards, and delivery..."

"I saw that..."

"When do you need this completed?"

"Our main location is a small space — a lobby, a reception area, his office, a kitchen, a file room, and a conference room..."

"That won't take 6 weeks..."

"That's good — but he has 4 other locations..."

"That's fine — we can do your office first — and if you're happy with us — which I'm sure you will be — we'll be happy to give your other locations a facelift..."

"Okay Ashley — thank you — you'll hear from us before the end of the week!"

"I'm looking forward to it..."

"Why are you smiling?" the director asked...

"Guess who just landed Heart Tech?"

"Are you serious?!"

"I'm serious!!"

"He has 5 locations!!"

"I know..."

"His commercial runs about 100 times a day!!"

"Commercial?"

"You haven't seen the new commercial for Kay Jewelers?!"

"Oh my God – that's him?!"

"That's him..." the director sighed...

"Yeesss!!!"

"Congratulations on your commission Ashley..."

"Oh my God!! I just got the down-payment for my house!! Thank you Lord!! Woo Hoo!!"

"Good morning My Queen..." Sid said as he sat down next to me and pulled me into a kiss...

"Good morning My King..."

"Who were you on the phone with?"

"I was on the phone with Uneebo..."

"Uneebo?"

"Yes – they do interior design for offices – I was on their website – I was thinking we could get our office done first and then we could give your other locations a facelift..."

"They don't need a facelift..."

"Yes they do..."

"You haven't even seen them to know they need a facelift – okay – let me take a look..." he said as he took the tablet from me... "Hmm... I like this..."

"I think your employees will like it too..."

"They don't really need it..."

"Yes they do..."

"They didn't have any damage done..."

"That's not it..."

"What is it then?"

"Look how bright and airy this is..."

"Okay..."

"As soon as they walk into work – this office will boost their morale and increase their productivity..."

"I didn't think of that..."

"A facelift will make them look forward to coming to work..."

"Okay – I'll do it..."

"Good – now let's take the quiz..."

"Quiz?"

"Yes – it gives them an idea of our design style..."

"How much is this going to cost?"

"It depends on the package – they have mini, the classic, and the premium..."

"We'll definitely get the mini for our office..."

"That's what I was thinking – the classic will be good for your other offices..."

"We'll get our office done first..."

"Yes — then we can go back to work and have a meeting with your reps — your reps can go back to their offices and share the information with your other employees..."

"That's a good idea..."

"Okay — now that I've taken care of that — let's talk about the wedding..."

"That's easy..." Sid breathed as he pushed me back on the couch and kissed me...

"Sid..."

"Mmm Hmm..."

"I... can't... talk..." I laughed in between kisses..."

"That's the point..." he breathed as he kissed me again...

"Sid... wait..."

"Okay..." he laughed as he pulled me back up..."

"I called the Taylor Inn Bed & Breakfast..."

"Okay..." he breathed as he began kissing my neck...

"Chris is going to help with the planning..."

"Uh huh..." he breathed as he took my breast out and began sucking on my nipple...

"Sid... Huh..."

"Are you done?"

"I'll tell you... later..." I panted as he pushed me back down on the couch and kissed between my breasts as he continued squeezing them... "Sid..." I moaned. I opened my legs and felt the head of his dick as he kissed my neck...

"You want it..."

"Yes..."

"Tell me..."

"I want it..."

"Again..." he breathed in my ear as he eased himself inside me..."

"I... want... it..."

"Again!" he growled as he started thrusting...

"Fuck... Yes... I want it!" I moaned as I grabbed his ass and pushed him in deeper...

"Shit..." he said as my phone rang...

"Who is it?" I panted...

"It's Chris..." he breathed...

"Don't stop..."

"Why... not?" he panted as he fucked me deeper...

"Huh... Sid..."

"Answer the phone..." he commanded...

"I... can't..."

"Here..." he breathed as he handed me the phone... "Answer it!!" he growled in my ear as he started thrusting again...

"H... Hello?"

"Hey Amber..."

"Hey..." I breathed. Sid was enjoying the way he was torturing me with slow, steady strokes...

"I heard back from Darryl..."

"Uh Huh..." Sid smiled at me as he squeezed my breasts and thrust up inside me hard...

"They can do 1 pm – is that too early for you?"

"Hold on – L'me ask Sid..." I said as I dropped the phone and pulled Sid down on top of me...

"Answer her..." he breathed in my ear...

"1 pm is... fine..."

"Okay – are you going to take care of the invites?"

"I'll take care of them..."

"Okay then – I'll talk to you soon..."

"Thanks' Chris..." I said as I hung up...

"Now... where were we?" Sid breathed in my ear...

"We... we're... right... here! Huh!" I moaned as I grabbed his ass and threw my pussy back at him as the crystals and spheres circled above us...

Chapter 39

"I can still smell smoke..." Sid said as we walked in...

"We won't have to worry about that too much longer..." I said...

"You sure you're okay?"

"Yes Sid..."

"So what are we doing in my office?"

"Well..." I answered as I walked over to him and put my arms around him... "We're going to take that wall down over there and make our office bigger..."

"Oh yea?" he breathed as he kissed me..."

"Yea..."

"What else..."

"Well... I'm getting a new desk..."

"Uh huh..."

"And we're getting a sectional..."

"A sectional?"

"Yes..." I breathed as I kissed him...

"Why?"

"Because... a sectional is bigger than a couch..."

"Yes... yes it is..."

"And... I can throw my leg up and the sectional will support it..."

"I see you've been doing your research..."

"Yes..."

"I'm looking forward to coming back to work..."

"So am I..." I breathed as I pulled him into a deep kiss. We stood in the office tonguing each other down until we heard a knock on the door...

"Who is it?" Sid answered...

"It's Ashley from Uneebo..."

"We'll be right there..." Sid said as he went to answer the door...

"Hello Mr. Heart – I'm Ashley – it's nice to meet you in person..."

"Thank you..."

"I'm Amber..." I said as I extended my hand...

"Hi Amber..." she greeted as she shook my hand... "I can't wait to get started – we need to brighten this up – it's very dreary..."

"I agree..." I said...

"I like gray..." Sid said...

"Gray is fine – but there's too much in this lobby – we need to bring in some sunlight – we'll get rid of this partition and put up a glass one – this will allow the sunlight to come in – we'll change out the lighting and we'll put a new desk out here..."

"I like that..." Sid agreed...

"Let's see your office..."

"C'mon..." Sid said as we followed him into his office...

"This is a good space – why do you want to take down that wall over there?"

"I want to make room for my desk..."

"Oh – you don't sit out there?"

"That area will be for our new Office Assistant..."

"Oh okay – that makes sense..."

"C'mon – I'll show you the kitchen..." Sid said as we followed him to the kitchen...

"This will be easy – you're not changing the layout so we can do this quick..."

"I just want it to stop looking like a doctor's office..." I laughed...

"Were any files damaged in the fire?" she asked as we went into the file room...

"No – we store most of our files electronically..." Sid answered...

"Okay – let's take a look at the conference room..." she said as we went inside... "Don't worry – I know this looks bad now – but once I'm done –

you won't remember what this looked like before..."

"That sounds good..." Sid said as he put his arm around me...

"I can't wait..." I sighed...

"We'll add a projector screen over there – you'll get a new table – new chairs – we'll put recessed lighting in the ceiling..."

"That sounds good..." Sid said...

"Where's your bathroom?"

"C'mon – I'll show you..." I answered as I hurried out the room and down the hall with Ashley following behind me...

"Oh my – we need to do something about this..." she said...

"What can we do?"

"We can change out these partitions – we can replace the toilets – the sinks – the mirrors – add new flooring, add a dyson hand dryer, and paint..."

"I love it!"

"Good – I'll get back to the office and get right on this..."

"Thank you Ashley..." I said as we came out the bathroom...

"I was getting ready to check on you..." Sid said...

"We're fine – Ashley was just telling me how she's going to give the bathroom a facelift..."

"As long as you don't turn it into a ladies room I'll be fine..." Sid laughed...

"Have a good day..." Ashley said as she opened the door to leave...

"You too..." Sid said as he closed the door...

"Come here..." he breathed as he pulled me into a hug and I broke down...

"Hey!!" Bazil greeted...

"Hey..." we both sighed...

"C'mon – let's go to my office..." We followed Bazil down to the office and Beautiee was excited to see us...

"Hey!!"

"Hey!!" we both exclaimed...

"What brings you here?" Beautiee asked...

"We set a wedding date..."

"Is this for the book?"

"You can put it in the book after we get married..."

"Oh shoot – okay – when are you getting married?"

"Friday – May 7th, at 1 p.m..."

"Where are you getting married?" Bazil asked...

"We're getting married at the Taylor Bed & Breakfast in Boston..."

"Nice!" Bazil exclaimed...

"We need you to be there early..." I said...

"You're inviting us to your wedding?!" Beautiee exclaimed...

"Yes..."

"I wonder if we'll get the same room..." Bazil asked...

"You've been there before?" Sid asked...

"My daughter was married there..."

"Oh wow!" Sid exclaimed...

"I gave birth to our son on their wedding night..." Beautiee sighed...

"Oh my God!" I exclaimed...

"We won't ever forget that place..." Bazil sighed...

"Darryl won't ever forget us!" Beautiee laughed...

"Hey Amber..."

"Hey Chris..."

"Are you okay?"

"I will be..."

"You sounded very strange earlier..."

"Oh that..." I laughed...

"Oh my God – no you didn't!!"

"Yea – we did..."

"Why didn't you let the call go to voicemail?!"

"Sid wouldn't let me..." I laughed...

"Oh my God – I can't with you two!!" she laughed...

"Thanks for not being mad..."

"I don't get mad – I get even..." she laughed...

"Oh shit – she said she's gonna get even Sid!!"

"Tell her bring it!!" Sid laughed...

"Okay – remember that!!" Chris laughed...

"We went to our building..." I sighed...

"How'd that go?"

"I thought I could handle it..."

"You probably need more time..."

"I'll be alright once Ashley is finished..."

"Ashley?"

"Yes – she does interior decorating for offices..."

"Oh that sounds nice!"

"She's from Uneebo..."

"I've never heard of them..."

"I'm glad Sid was with me..."

"Me too..."

"We went to invite Beautiee and Bazil to the wedding – and guess what?"

"What?"

"Their daughter got married at the Taylor Bed & Breakfast and Beautiee gave birth at the Bed & Breakfast on their wedding night!!"

"Wow – I bet Darryl will be happy to see them again!!" Chris laughed...

"I hope so..."

"I'm sure they will..."

"I want them to bring their kids to the wedding..."

"You do?"

"Yes – good thing I got the extra room..."

"I saw that..."

"I can't wait to get married..." I sighed...

"I can't wait to see you get married..."

"I'm going to lie down and take a nap – it's been a long day – I'll talk to you later..."

"Okay Amber – later..."

"Did I just here you say you were going to take a nap?" Sid asked...

"Yes..."

"Sounds good..." he said as he picked me up in his arms and carried me down the hallway to the bedroom...

Chapter 40

"Good morning – I'm Amber – follow me..." I said as they followed me down the hall...

"This is really nice..."
"I don't even recognize it..."
"Oh my God – you have an actual kitchen?"
"Look at the file room!"

"Good morning..." Sid greeted as they sat down at the table...
"Morning, morning..." they all said...
"This is Amber – Amber that's Scott, Tim, Cain, and William..."
"Nice to meet you all..." I said...

"Amber is going to be taking over the field..." Sid explained...

"Is Amber our new supervisor?" Scott asked...

"No – but she'll be the point person – you'll contact her and she'll refer new clients...

"So basically there won't be any changes..." Tim said...

"Yes – there will be changes – that's why you're here..." Sid answered...

"Are we being let go?" Cain asked...

"Hell no!" Sid laughed...

"Okay – I can breathe now..." William laughed...

"Here..." I said as I handed them each a shungite pendant...

"Umm... what's this?" Scott asked...

"That's a shungite pendant..."

"A what?" Tim asked...

"The pendant absorbs a lot of the magnetic energy from electronics..." I explained...

"So – we wear it?" Cain asked...

"I leave mine by the computer..." I answered...

"Okay..." William said...

"I've ordered these pendants for all your employees..." I explained...

"My wife has one of these..." Tim said...

"Really?" Sid asked...

"Yea – I just didn't know what it was..."

"Amber will be working with me so we're also hiring a new Office Assistant for us – and you'll each get a new Office Assistant..."

"Oh wow! Shelly will love that!" Scott exclaimed...

"You're going to get an increase in clients, so you'll need it..." Sid explained...

"I wish our office looked like this..." Cain said..."

"I'd love to bring new clients here..." William said...

"Your offices will look like this..." Sid explained...

"Really?" William asked...

"I wanted to give all the offices a facelift..." I answered...

"Are we getting a kitchen?" Scott asked...

"Yes..."

"Oh wow – I can't wait – when is all this happening?" Tim asked...

"Ashley from Uneebo will be contacting you directly – Stamford will be done first – followed by South Norwalk, Stratford, and then Milford..." I answered...

"How long will this take?" Scott asked...

"About 6 weeks..." I answered...

"Can we bring clients to Stamford until our offices are done?" William asked...

"If you guys can work out the scheduling so there's no hiccups – as long as our clients are happy..." Sid answered....

"Are they going to be working on all our offices at the same time?" Cain asked...

"I don't think so – Ashley will explain everything when she contacts you..." I answered...

"What do we do in the meantime?" William asked...

"Amber's going to send you a copy of the presentation – have a meeting with your staff and let them know what's coming..." Sid answered as he got up from the table...

"When will we get our new Office Assistants?"

"Amber will schedule the interviews and you'll come here for the interviews – we'll come to the conference room and we'll interview them together..."

"Oh shit – that might overwhelm the potential candidate..." Scott laughed...

"Then they won't work for us..." I said...

"Are you serious?"

"I'm serious – what would you do if you walked into a room for an interview and saw 6 people at the table?"

"Me?" Scott answered as he stood up and started walking around the table... "I'd work that mutha fucka – oh shit – excuse me!" he laughed...

"Exactly – I got set up like that when I interviewed for a position in the County Executive's Office for Westchester County..."

"Oh shit! They didn't tell you beforehand?" Sid asked...

"Nope..."

"Did you get the job?" Tim asked...

"Of course..." I laughed...

"You weren't nervous?"

"I was hella nervous – but they didn't know that..."

"We're growing and expanding – we don't need people that'd rather sit in the corner –if they can't handle being interviewed by us how will they handle clients coming in throughout the day in addition to the phones and other responsibilities?" Sid asked as he stood up...

"You're right..." Cain said...

"C'mon – let's go to my office..." Sid said as he left the conference room and we all followed him to his office...

"Oh my God! This is nice!" Tim exclaimed...

"Where'd you get those spheres?" William asked...

I have a friend that sells them..." I answered...

"Can you put me in touch with your friend?"

"Sure..."

"Okay – I want you all to make sure you go to the bathroom before you leave..." Sid said...

"Really Sid?" Scott laughed...

"Yes..."

"Yes Sir!" Cain laughed as they all went into the bathroom...

"Oh shit!" we heart Tim exclaim as we waited outside the door...

"Yo Sid..." Cain said as he snatched the door open... "We're getting a new bathroom too?!"

"Yea..." he laughed...

"Thank God – and thank you – no offense – but our bathroom is ugly as hell!!" William laughed...

"That's pretty much what Ashley said..." I laughed...

Chapter 41

"Hey Chris..."

"Wait a minute – where's Sid?'

"He's in bed..."

"And you are in bed with him?"

"No Chris..." I laughed...

"Okay – what can I do for you?"

"How'd you like to help me pick out a wedding dress?"

"I'd love to – Chandra will be home so I won't have to worry about Maui..."

"Can Chandra come too? We can make it a ladies day..."

"Oh that sounds like fun – what time did you want to go?"

"Doesn't matter..."

"Okay – we'll meet at David's Bridal at 2..."

"Good morning..." Sid said as he came into the living room..."

"Good morning..."

"I don't like waking up without you waking up next to me..."

"I'm sorry My King – I didn't want to disturb you while you were sleeping..."

"That's not true..."

"Yes it is..."

"The truth is you didn't want me to hear your conversation with Chris..." he said as he smiled at me mischievously...

"Yes..." I sighed...

"What time are you leaving?"

"Chris wants me to meet her at 2..."

"Good – that gives you time to make it up to me..." he said as he took my hand and led me into the bathroom...

"I want Beautiee and Bazil to bring their kids to the wedding..."

"Really?"

"Yes – I think it will be nice for them to remember the night their son was born..."

"Okay – I'll tell him..." he said as he turned on the water, pulled the curtain aside, and helped me into the shower...

"Hey Bazil – you busy?"

"Always – but I have some time – what can I do for you?"

"Amber went with Chris to pick out a wedding dress..."

"Oh... that's nice..."

"I need your help..."

"I gotchu – what time can you get here?"

"I can get to you by 2..."

"Okay – see you when you get here..."

"Welcome to David's Bridal – May I help you?"

"I'm getting married on Friday, May 7th..." I answered...

"Will you need dresses as well?" the assistant asked Chris and Chandra...

"I won't need a dress – but if you have any pant suits I'd like to see those..." Chris answered...

"I'd love to see what you have in dresses..." Chandra answered...

"Will you be wearing a white dress?"

"Yes..." I answered...

"About what size are you?"

"I'm a size 8..."

"Dresses for you are to the right – ladies – dresses and pant suits are to the left – my name is Lisa – take your time – when you're ready I'll come assist you..."

"Thank you Lisa..." I said...

"Oh my God – there's too many dresses..." Chandra laughed...

"I'll help you..." Chris said... "Did you look at the website?"

"Yes – but there's so many!"

"Okay – I think I know what you'd like..." Chris said as she started looking at dresses...

"Nope... Nope... Nope..." Chandra kept saying as she shook her head back and forth. Chris just ignored her and continued looking at dresses... "That's it!"

"Oh that's pretty!" I exclaimed...

"Hmm – High-Neck Satin A-Line – navy blue – okay – I'll take it off the rack right now before anybody else can see it..." Chris said...

"Babe – did you check to see if it's my size?"

"I know what size you wear..." Chris laughed...

"Where are you going?" Chandra asked...

"I'm going to see if they have that navy blue pants suit over there in my size..." Chris answered as she went over to the aisle with the pant suits and saw what she wanted. We got up and just as we got there, Chris took the pant suit off the rack...

"Ohhh... that bustier is sexy..." Chandra breathed...

"I know..." Chris agreed as she smiled at her mischievously. I smiled to myself as I remembered her promise to get even...

"Okay Amber – Are you ready to pick out a dress?"

"Yes I am..." I sighed...

"Okay then!" Chris exclaimed as we went over to where the dresses were hanging and started going through them...

"This is nice..." Chandra said as she showed me her pick...

"Naa..." I answered as I shook my head...

"How 'bout this one?" Chris asked as she showed me her pick...

"Mmmm... No..." I answered as I shook my head. We kept looking and then I found it... "This is it!" I exclaimed...

"Oh that's pretty!" Chris exclaimed...

"I like it..." Chandra agreed...

"I love it..." I sighed as I took the Oleg Cassini Long Sleeve Beaded Lace Folded Skirt Wedding Dress off the rack and looked to see if it was my size... "It's my size..."

"Go try it on!" Chris exclaimed...

"Come with me – I need help..." I said...

"Okay – c'mon..." Chris said as she started to follow me to the dressing room...

"Chandra – you coming?"

"Oh – you want me to come too – okay – sure!" Chandra exclaimed as she got up and we went inside the dressing room. After they helped me put the dress on, I came out wearing the wedding dress, I stood in front of the mirror... and I started crying...

"What's wrong?" Chris asked... "You don't like it?"

"Oh my God... this is my dress..."

"Yes it is..." Chandra said...

"C'mon – let's get this dress off..." Chris said as Lisa came over...

"How's it going?"

"She found her dress..." Chandra answered...

"Oh wow – you look beautiful! Do you want the veil, the pearl earrings, and the pearl bracelet as well?"

"Yes..."

"Okay then – you'll need three pairs of shoes..."

"Why do I need three pair of shoes?"

"You need one to wear while you're getting ready, one for the ceremony, and one for the reception..."

"I'll just take two pair – I don't need shoes to wear while I'm getting ready..."

"Okay – here's our catalog of wedding shoes – personally I think you should go with the High-Heeled Sandals with Crystal Flower Strap by Vera Wang – they'll bring out the beads in your dress and show off your pedicure..."

"I love them!"

"Okay – now you'll definitely want to be comfortable at the reception – here's our catalog of wedges and flats..."

"I want these!" I yelled as I pointed at the Crystal-Topped Wedge Sandals with Ankle Strap...

"Nice choice!" I'll put everything up front with your name on it – what's your name?"

"Amber..."

"Okay Amber..." Lisa said as she took everything up front...

"Okay Chris – try on your pant suit!" I exclaimed...

"You need any help with that bustier?" Chandra asked...

"As a matter of fact – I do..." Chris answered as she smiled at Chandra mischievously...

"I'll be right there..." Chandra said as she got up and they both went into the dressing room...

"I can't wait until their wedding night..." Chris said as she started getting undressed..."

"I love weddings..." Chandra said...

"I love weddings too..."

"Chris..." Chandra said as she helped Chris get into the bustier... "I want to renew our wedding vows..."

"We can do that..."

"Really? Wow – that was easy..."

"I'll marry you as many times as you want me to..." she breathed as she pulled Chandra into a kiss...

"See – Amber's going to come looking for us if we don't hurry up..." Chandra laughed...

"It would serve her right too – I still owe them – and they told me to bring it..."

"Chris – are you serious?"

"Don't worry Chandra – we won't do it here – plus it won't be as much fun without Sid..." she explained as she put the pants on...

"Oh thank God!" Chandra laughed...

"Had you worried huh?" Chris laughed...

"Well – I guess we could lock the door – but you're right – It won't be as much fun – we need to wait for Sid..."

"C'mon..." Chris said as they both came out the dressing room and Chris modeled the pant suit...

"Oh my damn! You're rocking the hell out of that suit! And that bustier!" I exclaimed...

"Thank you Amber..."

"You look good Babe..."

"Thank you Chandra..." Chris said... "I'm definitely taking this..."

"Okay – time for me to try on my dress!" Chandra exclaimed...

"Let's go..." Chris said as she held the door open for Chandra and they went back into the dressing room...

"I swear..." Chris laughed... "I almost wanna do something just to fuck with Amber!"

"I got it!" Chandra exclaimed...

"What?"

"Well – Amber's always saying how she wants us to do a live show in the backyard – let's do a live show in the backyard – when the show's over, we can invite them to spend the night – and then we can put on a show for them..."

"Oh yes – I love that idea – I'll burn some sage – and we'll play with some lepidolite so we get natural lithium before we get started!" Chris laughed...

"Okay – let's go see how this looks on me..." Chandra said as they both came out the dressing room...

"Ooohhh Chandra! You look beautiful!" I exclaimed...

"That dress was made for you..." Chris said...

"Thank you Amber, thanks, Babe..."

"Oh my – that dress looks great on you..." Lisa said as she came over...

"Thank you..." Chandra said...

"Okay Ladies – I know you want comfortable shoes..." Lisa laughed as she showed Chris the catalog...

"I want these right here..." she said as she pointed to the Pink Paradox Strappy Shimmer T-Strap Mules...

"What size?"

"Size 8..."

"Okay – how about you?" Lisa asked as she showed the catalog to Chandra...

"I'll take these right here..." Chandra answered as she pointed to the Wendie Glitter Peep Toe Wedge...

"And what size do you need?"

"Size 6..."

"Okay Ladies... now that you've picked out your dresses and your accessories – it's time to let the bride prepare for her wedding night..." Lisa said...

"Okay – let me get out of this dress and then we can go take a look..." Chandra said...

"We'll meet you up front..." Chris said as they went into the dressing room...

"Here's a sample of everything we have in the glass cases – take your time – if you see something you like – let me know and I'll go get it..." Lisa said as she walked away to help another customer...

"We need something for your wedding night too..." Chris laughed...

"I like almost everything in here..." I said as I looked through the cases...

"Take your time – pick what you want – we have all afternoon..." Chris said...

"Okay – I want this All Over Beaded Vintage Inspired Garter..."

"Oh that's pretty..." Chris said...

"It sure is..." Chandra agreed...

"Do you want anything else?" Chris asked...

"Hmmm... I do like this Personalized Glitter Print Mrs. Satin Robe in red..."

"Ooohhh – I like it too – and it comes in large – that's perfect for me too..." Chandra said...

"Okay – I'll get us one in fuchsia..." Chris said...

"Thanks' Babe..."

"You're welcome..."

"How's everything going?" Lisa asked as she came over...

"Everything fine – we're ready..." I said as I handed her a list...

"Okay – thanks for writing this list for me – I see you have 1 robe in snall/medium - how would you like this personalized?"

"I'd like it personalized as Mrs. Heart..." I answered...

"And how would you like these personalized?" Lisa asked Chris and Chandra...

"C & C..." Chris answered...

"Both of them?"

"Yes..." Chandra answered...

"Okay – I'll take care of everything – go get your car and bring it to the front – I want to get everything in the car before the guys get here..."

"The guys?" I asked...

"Yes – your fiancée is on his way – and we can't let your fiancée see anything before your wedding..."

"Oh wow – that's great – everyone can get taken care of here – I didn't know you could take care of the guys – I thought David's Bridal was just for Ladies!" I laughed...

"Yes – now go get your car – and I'll make sure everything's personalized correctly..." Lisa said as she hurried off...

"Thank you for calling David's Bridal – this is Lisa... Yes Mr. Heart – we'll see you soon..." Lisa said as she hung up...

"C'mon –let's get outta here!" I exclaimed as Lisa loaded everything into the car and we drove back towards Bridgeport...

Chapter 42

"I ordered a car for us – he should be outside now..." Bazil said as he went to the door... "It's here – let's go..." Bazil said as he opened the door and they got in the limousine...

"Where we goin' first?" Sid asked...

"We're going to David's Bridal..." Bazil answered...

"Isn't that for Women?"

"It's for Men too..." Bazil answered...

"Hmmm... okay... I need some coffee..." Sid said...

"You need some Henney!" Bazil laughed...

"Mr. Osgood – we're here – would you like for me to wait in the parking lot for you?"

"Yes Mike..." Bazil answered...

"Okay – do you mind if I park, go get something to eat – and come right back?"

"That's fine Mike…"

"Okay – thank you Mr. Osgood – I'll let you out…" he said as he got out and opened the door for them…"

"You ready Sid?" Bazil asked…

"Oh Yea… " he sighed as they went inside…

"Mr. Osgood – welcome back – it'll be my pleasure to take care of your wedding needs – who's the lucky groom?"

"This is Obsidian Heart – he's…"

"He's the one from the commercial! Oh my God – I can't believe it – you're fiancée was just here – I can't believe I didn't recognize her!" Lisa laughed…

"Nice to meet you…" Sid said as he shook her hand…

"I'm Lisa - I'm going to love this…" she said as she ran her hands down Sid's shoulders and across his chest…

"Is this how you greet all your male customers?" Sid asked…

"Oh my goodness – I'm sorry – I didn't mean to offend you – I was just taking a quick measurement – everyone else uses measuring tape but I'm usually pretty accurate by feeling my way around…" she laughed…

"It's a good thing my wife isn't here – the last time I told her I had women all over me she didn't like it..." Sid laughed...

"Women all over you?" Bazil asked...

"I'll tell you about it later..." Sid laughed...

"C'mon guys – let's get you in and out..." she said as she took them in the back to the men's section... "We have complete packages starting at $99.00..." she said as they started looking at suits... "We have Black by Vera Wang and Joseph Abound – personally I think Joseph Abound is the right choice for you..."

"Why?" Sid asked...

"Black men are built different – you have broad chests and shoulders – white men are more straight up and down with small, round butts..."

"Okay!" Sid laughed...

"When you've been feeling men as long as I have – you get to know all the shapes and sizes..." Lisa laughed...

"What colors do you have?" Sid asked...

"We have black, gray, and navy..."

"I'd like navy..." Sid said...

"Okay – I'll be back with the suit and the accessories – what size shoe do you wear?"

"I'm a nine..."

"Okay – I'll be right back..."

"Nice choice..." Bazil said...

"Thanks..."

"Here you are..." Lisa said as she came back with everything..."

"Hmmm... a pink tie..." Sid said...

"Try it on – it looks great with the navy – and it'll also go great with your complexion..."

"Thank you – I'll be right back..." Sid said as he went into the dressing room...

"Oh wow..." Bazil said when Sid came out and stood in front of the mirror...

"You look great!" Lisa said...

"I'll take everything..." Sid said...

"Okay – I'll bring these items up front and I'll be right back..." she said as she took the items to the front...

"Have you decided what you'd like?" Lisa asked Bazil...

"I still have the Monaco Quartz black suit from my wedding..." Bazil answered...

"You came to David's Bridal for your wedding?" Sid asked...

"Yes..."

"Where were you married?"

"In Vegas..."

"Oh nice! They have a David's Bridal in Vegas?"

"Yes they do..."

"Okay – we have some other accessories here in the glass case – if you see anything you like, just let me know..." she said as she went to put everything in bags...

"I like this Kimono Robe..." Sid said...

"Get it..." Bazil said...

"Okay..." Sid said...

"Okay – what name would you like?" Lisa asked...

"King Obsidian for the black one – Queen Amber for the white one..."

"Okay – it'll be a little while to get your items customized – you guys wanna go out for a bit and come back?"

"Naa... we'll wait..." Bazil answered...

"You sure? It's gonna be about an hour..."

"Okay – we'll come back..." Bazil answered... "C'mon – let's get outta here for a bit..." Bazil said as he went out and Sid followed him to the limousine...

"Hey guys – how'd everything go?" Mike asked...

"Everything's fine Mike..." Bazil answered as they got in the limousine...

"You headed back home?"

"Not yet..."

"Where shall I take you next?"

"Andinis..."

"Okay Mr. Osgood – Andinis it is..."Mike said as they drove off towards the restaurant...

"Welcome to Andinis – nice to see you again Mr. Osgood – right this way..." the hostess said as she took them to the table... "The waitress will be here to take your orders – we have some new items on the menu..." the hostess said...

"Hello Mr. Osgood – nice to see you again..." Carmen said as she came over to the table... "May I start you off with some appetizers?"

"Yes – we'll have my usual..." Bazil answered...

"Risotto Balls, Veal Meatballs, Rabe & Sausage, Fried Calamari – and Samuel Adams – right?"

"Yes on the appetizers – but instead of Samuel Adams – we'll take Henney on the rocks......"

"Okay – I'll be back with your drinks and appetizers..." she said as she went to place the order. Carmen came back with their drinks and put them on the table...

"Congratulations..." Bazil said as he raised his glass...

"Thanks Bazil..." Sid said...

"I'm happy for you..."

"I just hope I got it right this time..." Sid sighed...

"Tell me about these women..." Bazil said as they sipped...

"Here are your appetizers..." Carmen said as she placed them on the table... "Can I get you refills?"

"Yes – please..." Bazil said...

"Coming right up..." Carmen said as she took their glasses and then went to get them both refills... "Here's your drinks..." Carmen said as she put their drinks on the table... "Are you guys ready to order?"

"We'll have the NY Strip Steak..." Bazil answered...

"Regular or Cesar?"

"Regular..."

"Okay – pasta or baked potato?"

"Baked potato..."

"How would you like your steak?"

"Medium well..."

"Does that work for you?" she asked Sid...

"I'd like well done..." Sid answered...

"Okay – medium well, well-done – I'll be back..." Carmen said as she walked away...

"When I went to see Jade, the woman recognized me from the commercial..."

"Ohhh... I see..." Bazil laughed...

"They went crazy..."

"I bet they did..."

"I told the guard to let me speak to Jade in private and then I'd take pictures after – Jade made me so mad I almost forgot..."

"What happened?"

"I'm trying to forget..." Sid sighed...

"That bad?"

"She had an abortion..."

"Sid – why didn't you tell me?"

"Please don't tell Beautiee..."

"I won't..."

"She told me she had an abortion because she didn't want to explain to her son that she was in jail for trying to kill his other Mommy..."

"Does Amber know?"

"She knows..."

"I'm glad she was there for you..."

"I saw my son..." Sid said as he started tearing up..."

"You saw him?"

"My mother came to see me – she told me I don't have to worry about him because she got him... and my son spoke to me..."

"Oh wow – Sid – I'm sorry..."

"He said don't worry Daddy – I'm with grandma..."

"Oh my God – that's beautiful... and sad..."

"I told Obi I loved him... and he said I loved you too Daddy..."

"Okay stop – we're supposed to be celebrating your wedding to Amber..." Bazil said as he wiped his eyes...

"That reminds me – Amber wants you and Beautiee to bring your kids to our wedding..."

"Really?"

"Yes – she wants to remind you of the night your son was born..."

"That's sweet – I'll be sure and let Beautiee know..."

"Amber asked me how many children I want..."

"How many do you want?"

"I don't know – but she asked me if that meant she was having another baby and I said yes..."

"I remember the first week Beautiee was home from the hospital – she was horny – and I was scared!" Bazil laughed...

"You? Scared?"

"She just had a baby – I didn't want to hurt her – I went slow at first – but once I got inside – oh my God!"

"It was on and poppin' like that?!"

"Let me say this – if you think Amber's pussy is good now – wait until she has the baby..."

"Oh damn!"

"Pregnancy is the best thing to happen to pussy!" Bazil laughed...

"Amber's not showing yet..."

"You're in for it..." Bazil said as Carmen brought their food to the table...

"Here's your steaks – one medium well – one well done – baked potatoes, and salads – can I get you anything else?" Carmen asked...

"Yea – A1!" Sid answered...

"I'll be back..." Carmen said...

"So I'm in for it?"

"Oh yea – I didn't want to cum but Beautiee wasn't tryin' to hear that – I asked her what if you get pregnant and she said what if I do?"

"Oh wow – I see why you have 4 kids..."

"I'd have more if she wanted them..."

"You love kids?"

"Always have..."

"Amber told me my daughter's name will be Princess – and my son's name will be Prince..."

"Oh so she's already planning to give you a son..."

"Yea..."

"Here's the A1 – Enjoy..." Carmen said as she put the jar on the table and went to help another table...

"Oh this is good!" Sid smacked...

"Can your wife cook steak?"

"Oh yea – but I do the cooking in my house..." Bazil said...

"Your wife can't cook?"

"I won't let her..."

"Why?"

"I love cooking for her..."

"Aww – I told Amber I can cook anything she wants..."

"Really? When are we gonna taste your cooking?"

"I'll invite you over for dinner after we get settled..."

"Well..." Bazil said as he rubbed his stomach... "I guess we better go get our things before they think we forgot..."

"Oh my God..." Sid laughed as he got up and stretched... "I'm so full!" Sid exclaimed as he got up...

"Thank you Mr. Osgood – always a pleasure..." Carmen said as she put the check on the table...

"You're welcome – I'll see you again..." Bazil said as he signed the receipt and they got up to leave...

"You didn't give her anything...." Sid said...

"They have my card on file..." Bazil said...

"Ooohhh..." Sid said as they went outside and got back in the limousine...

"Back to David's Bridal?" Mike asked...

"Yes Mike..."

"Okay Mr. Osgood..." Mike said as they drove off...

"Mr. Osgood – I was just getting ready to call you..." Lisa said as they walked in...

"Is everything ready?" Bazil asked...

"Yes - everything's ready for you to take to the car – if you have any problems or you need anything – you can call me directly..."

"Thank you Lisa..." Bazil said...

"You're welcome Mr. Osgood – have a great day – and congratulations Mr. Heart..."

"Would you like to take a picture with me?"

"Can I?"

"Sure..." he said as he put his arm around her... "Give me your phone..."

"Okay!" she squealed as she handed the phone to him and he took a selfie...

"Thank you!"

"You're welcome – have a good day..." he said as they went outside...

"Mike – I'm going home – and then I'd like you to drop Sid off in Bridgeport..." Bazil said...

"Okay Mr. Osgood..." Mike said as he drove off. When they got to the house, Mike opened the door, Bazil got out, and took out his bags...

"Thanks Bazil..." Sid said...

"You're welcome – I'll see you soon..." Bazil said as he went inside...

"Daddy!" they all squealed as they ran towards him...

"Hey!" Bazil exclaimed as he hugged them...

"How'd everything go?" Beautiee asked...

"It was okay..."

"Just okay?"

"I got another tux – Sid wanted me to wear navy blue..."

"Doesn't matter what you wear – you won't have it on that long..." Beautiee breathed as she pulled him into a kiss...

"Okay Your Majesty – where to?" Mike asked...

"Why are you calling me that?" Sid asked...

"I recognize you from the commercial..."

"Oh okay – I'm going to Lafayette Avenue in Bridgeport..."

"Yes Your Majesty..." Mike said...

Chapter 43

"Where are we going now?" Chris asked...

"Boca Oyster Bar!" I answered as we got in the car...

"Welcome to Boca – table for 3?"

"Yes..." I answered...

"Right this way..." the hostess said as she escorted us to a table out by the water...

"This is nice..." Chandra said...

"Thank you for coming Chandra..." I said

"You're welcome – thank you for inviting me..."

"Welcome to Boca – my name is Tamika – may I start you off with something to drink?"

"Sangrias or Margaritas?" I asked...

"Sangrias!" they both exclaimed...

"Sangrias it is..." the waitress said as she wrote that down... "Would you like any appetizers?"

"Yes – we'll have fried calamari, clams casino, boca ceviche, and filet tips..." I answered...

"Okay – I'll be right back with your drinks..." the waitress said as she walked away...

"This is the perfect ending to a great day..." Chris sighed...

"It sure is..." I sighed...

"Here's your drinks – your appetizers will be out shortly..." the waitress interrupted as she put the drinks on the table and walked away...

"To Amber..." Chris said as she raised her glass...

"To Amber..." Chandra said as she raised her glass...

"To all of us..." I said as I raised my glass and we clinked...

"This is how we do it!" we all sang and then we took a sip...

"Here's your appetizers..." the waitress interrupted as she began putting the food on the table...

"That looks really good..." Chris said...

"If you need anything else, I'll be over there..." the waitress said as she pointed across the area...

"Thank you..." I said. When the waitress walked away, we started helping ourselves...

"Oh my God – this is sooo good!" Chandra exclaimed...

"I love coming here..." I said...

"I could eat here every day..." Chris said...

"How's everything?" the waitress asked...

"Delicious..." I answered...

"Are you ready to order your entrée?"

"I am..." I answered...

"So are we..." Chandra answered...

"Okay – what would you like?"

"I'd like the lobster ravioli..." I answered...

"Ravioli?" Chandra asked...

"Absolutely – it has lobster, shrimp, scallops, peas, and red roasted peppers – in a cream sauce..." I answered...

"I'm having the cioppino – it has lobster, shrimp, scallops, clams, calamari, and plum tomato white wine sauce – over linguine al dente..." Chris answered...

"Ooohhh – that sounds good!" Chandra exclaimed... "I'll have that too..."

"Okay – I'll go place your order..." the waitress said as she walked away...

"So how's everything been between you two?" Chris asked...

"We already know about the sex!' Chandra laughed...

"I've been busy – in a good way..." I answered...

"That's good to hear..." Chris said...

"I'll be going back to work after we're married..."

"You're not going on a honey moon?" Chandra asked...

"We never talked about it..."

"How do you get married without talking about a honey moon?" Chandra asked...

"Well – we didn't do it on purpose – I was so busy planning the wedding, having the office re-decorated, setting up interviews – we just haven't had time to talk about a honeymoon – plus – we need a bigger place..."

"Do you want to go on a honeymoon?" Chris asked...

"I feel like I'm already on a honeymoon..."

"That's not the same thing..." Chandra said...

"Here's your entrees – let me know if you need anything else..." the waitress said as she put our food on the table..."

"I know it's not – but I'm okay for the moment..." I said as I started eating my ravioli...

"This is soooo good!" Chandra exclaimed as she started eating...

"I told you!" Chris said and then we continued eating...

"This is perfect..." Sid said as he looked on their website... "18 days – Grand Tour of Europe: London to Rome with Florence extension..." he read...

"Two nights in London, two nights in Paris, sightseeing tour of Paris, two nights in Amsterdam, one night in Heidelberg Region via Cologne & Rhine River cruise, two nights Swiss Alps, one day sightseeing tour of Lucerne, 1 night Lake Como Region, boat ride on Lake Como, two nights in Venice, sightseeing tour of Venice, two nights in Rome, two nights in Florence – this is perfect – June 18th to July 5th..." he read out loud as he booked it... "I hope Amber doesn't mind waiting to go on our honeymoon..." he sighed as he entered all the information, paid for the trip, and waited to receive the confirmation in his email...

"Is everything alright?" the waitress asked...

"Everything's fine..." I sighed...

"I'll bring the check..." the waitress said as she walked away...

"This was so good – I'm glad we came..." Chris said...

"So am I..." Chandra said...

"Here you go – have a great evening..." the waitress said as she put the check on the table...

"Here you go..." Chris said as she handed the waitress the bill holder with her credit card...

"Thank you!" I exclaimed...

"You're welcome..." Chris said. When we got home, we got out the car and I thought we were going to go upstairs...

"We're going to leave from here – we have a long drive ahead of us..." Chris said...

"Thank you both so much..." I said as we all hugged...

"You're welcome – we'll see you Friday..." Chris said...

"See you Friday..." I said as they got in their car and drove off...

Chapter 44

Wedding Eve
Thursday, May 6th, 2021

"My Queen... we need to talk..." Sid sighed...

"Yes My King?" I asked as I looked in his eyes...

"Come sit with me..."

"Okay..." I sighed. Sid had a serious look on his face and I wondered what could be troubling him a few hours before our wedding...

"I need to ask you something..."

"Yes, I'll marry you..."

"I'm serious..."

"So am I..."

"Once we're married..."

"Yes My King?"

"I don't know how to say it..."

"Is there something you need from me?"

"Yes..."

"Tell me..."

"I've been holding back..."

"From me?"

"Yes..."

"Why?"

"Do you remember what happened in my office?"

"Yes..."

"You told me no..."

"I did..."

"You said you wanted me..."

"I did want you..."

"Were you afraid of me?"

"My King..." I said as I took his face in my hands... "I wasn't afraid of you..."

"So... are you saying I don't have to hold back?"

"You haven't been holding back..." I laughed...

"Yes... I have..."

"Do you remember the scene in Game of Thrones where Daenerys asked the other woman to help her please her husband?"

"Yes..."

"Do you remember how he wanted to take her from behind and she stopped him?"

"Yes..."

"He thought she didn't want him – but after she pushed him down on his back so she could look in his face while they made love, he realized he didn't need to hold back at all – she became his sun and he became her moon..."

"I remember that too..." he breathed as he pushed me down on my back and lay on top of me...

"Sid... wait..."

"What did you say?" he laughed as he sat up...

"It's just a few more hours – I wanna go to bed, get some sleep, and dream about my wedding night..."

"Okay... we'll wait..." he breathed as he helped me up and pulled me into a kiss... "But it's going to cost you..." he said as he took me by the hand and pulled me down the hall towards the bedroom...

"Sid – look!!"

"I've never seen them like this!!" he exclaimed as we watched the crystals and spheres form a T in the ceiling...

"Take off your clothes..." I commanded...

"I thought you wanted to wait..." he laughed...

"Take off your clothes!"

"Yes My Queen..." he laughed as he stripped...

"Get on the bed on your back! Sid did as he was told... "Put your arms out at your sides and open your legs...

"Yes My Queen..." he laughed as he did as he was told. It took everything in me not to jump on his dick as it sprang to attention... "Oh wow..." he whispered as the crystals and spheres came closer to his body and spun above him...

"They're aligning your chakras..." I whispered as I started crying...

"Get my phone..." I got his phone and began recording. Sid cried along with me as the crystals and spheres moved in unison up and down his arms, his legs, and his torso, spinning and glowing for about 25 minutes, until they floated back up to the ceiling but they remained in a T formation. Sid got up off the bed, came over to me, and took the phone... "Take off your clothes..."

"Yes My King..." I breathed as I stripped...

"Get on the bed..."

"Yes My King..." I said as I got on the bed on my back, put my arms out at my sides, and opened my legs...

"Oh my God..." Sid whispered as he started recording. We both cried as the crystals and spheres moved in unison up and down my arms, my legs, and my torso... "I wonder if my daughter can feel their energy..." he whispered...

"She can..." I whispered... "She hasn't stopped moving..."

"Show me..." he whispered as he sat down on the bed...

"Look..." I whispered as Sid looked at my stomach...

"My daughter..." he whispered as he held the phone in one hand and touched my stomach with the other... "Hey Princess... I'm your father..." he whispered...

"Oohh... that tickles..." I laughed. Sid continued recording until the crystals and spheres floated back into the display case and then he put the phone down...

"Get dressed..."

"Where are we going?" I laughed...

"We're going to bed..."

"I don't understand..."

"You said you wanted to wait..."

"I do..."

"If you don't hurry up and put some clothes on – I'm not waiting..."

"Yes My King!" I laughed as I jumped up off the bed and started getting dressed. Sid got dressed along with me and when we both got back on the bed, he deliberately pulled me close to him so I could feel his dick pressing up against me...

"I'm giving you fair warning..." he breathed in my ear... "Once we say I do..." he breathed again as he nibbled on my earlobe... "I'm going to make you scream..."

Wedding Day
Friday, May 7th, 2021, 1 p.m.

"Welcome everyone!" Darryl said as we all went inside...

"Darryl – it's nice to see you again..." Bazil said...

"Nice to see you too – is there going to be another baby born tonight?" Darryl laughed...

"I'm not pregnant..." Beautiee laughed...

"Hey!" Darryl exclaimed as he hugged her...

"Hi Darryl – this is our son Jay – he's the one that was born here..." Beautiee said as she introduced him..."

"Hi Mr. Darryl..." Jay said...

"Oh my God – hello!"

"Mommy – was I really born here?" Jay asked...

"Yes Jay..." Beautiee answered...

"Mr. Darryl – this is my brother Joseph..." Jay said as he introduced him...

"Hello Joseph..." Darryl greeted as he shook Joseph's hand...

"And these are my sisters – this is Joy, and this is Lydia..."

"Oh my word! You are so beautiful!" Darryl exclaimed...

"Thank you..." Joy and Lydia said...

"Were we born here too Mommy?" Joy asked...

"No – Jay was the only one..." Beautiee answered...

"How come I wasn't born here?" Joseph asked...

"When I was pregnant with your brother, your sister Starr was getting married to Chandler – I didn't know I was going to have Jay early..." Beautiee explained...

"I was born early? In the morning?" Jay asked...

"No Jay – Mommy was supposed to carry you in her tummy for 9 months – but you were born after 8 months..." Bazil explained...

"Why did I come so early?" Jay asked...

"I think it was because you were excited to see your sister on her wedding day..." Beautiee answered...

"Oh okay..." Jay said...

'I'm Sid – the groom – and this is my bride – Amber..."

"Nice to meet you both..." Darryl said...

"These are my best friends – Chris, her wife Chandra, and their dog, Maui..." I said...

"Nice to meet you both – and very nice to meet you Maui – are you a good dog?" he asked as he bent down to pet her...

"Aww..." we all sighed as Maui gave him kisses...

"C'mon – let's get you to your rooms so you can get ready for the wedding..." Darryl said as we all followed him... "Jay – this is the room you were born in – you're going to sleep here with your brother and sisters..."

"Aww..." I sighed along with Sid, Chris and Chandra...

"I like this room!" Jay exclaimed...

"We did too..." Beautiee sighed...

"Your parent's will be sleeping in this room right next door to you..." Darryl said as we all followed him to the next room...

"This is nice!" Chris exclaimed...

"It sure is!" Chandra agreed...

"I can't wait to go to bed..." Bazil said as he smiled as Beautiee mischievously...

"Your rooms are upstairs..." Darryl said as he started upstairs...

"Bazil – you comin'?" Sid asked...

"I'll meet you in the dressing room..." Bazil answered...

"Okay – let's go upstairs – I wanna see our room!" I exclaimed...

"Well c'mon!" Darryl exclaimed. We followed him upstairs and when we got to our room, I was in awe...

"Oh my God..." I whispered...

"This room is perfect..." Sid said...

"Oh my God – this room is so elegant..." Chris said...

"I can't wait to see our room..." Chandra said...

"Right this way..." Darryl said as we all followed him to their room...

"Oh Chris..." Chandra exclaimed...

"It's beautiful..." Chris agreed...

"Okay – I'm going to go downstairs and get everything ready – I'll see you all at 1 p.m..." Darryl said as he went downstairs...

"Okay ladies – let's go!" Chris said...

"I'm coming!" I squealed as hurried into the dressing room...

"Amber – I need you to take these bags to your room and come right back – we need to get your hair done and get you ready for your husband..."

"Okay!" I squealed as I grabbed the bags and ran to our room...

"Aiight Sid – let's go!" Bazil said as he came upstairs...

"Where are we going?" Sid asked...

"In the other dressing room..." Darryl's assistant said as he stuck his head out the room...

"You ready Sid?" Bazil asked as they all went into the room...

"Yea..." Sid sighed...

"Me too..." Bazil said as he pulled Sid into a hug...

"I'm a nervous wreck..."

"I cried right along with Beautiee..." Bazil said as they started getting ready...

"Let me tell you what happened last night..."

"I heard enough on the phone!" Chris laughed...

"What happened on the phone?" Chandra asked...

"She called when we were having sex and

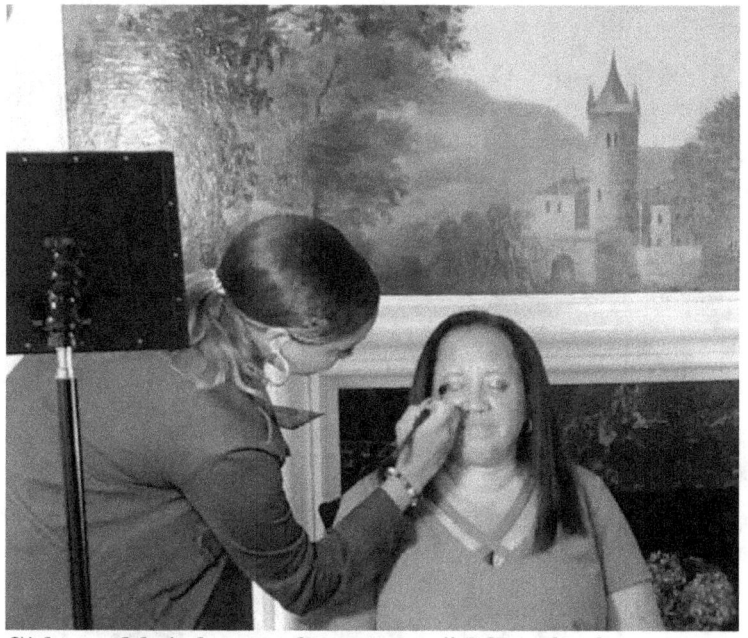

Sid wouldn't let me hang up..." I laughed...

"He wouldn't let you? How does that even – you know what – never mind..." Chandra laughed...

"We stopped – well – we kinda stopped..." I laughed...

"Oh my God – I would've hung up the phone..." Chandra laughed...

"So what happened last night?" Chris asked...

"We went to bed and the crystals and spheres were spinning and floating above us in a

T formation..."

"Ooohhh – chakra alignment..." Chris sighed...

"Yes!" I exclaimed...

"How did they align your chakras from the ceiling?!" Chandra asked...

"They didn't – they hovered on top of us and spun up and down our arms, our legs, and our torsos..." I explained...

"Oh wow..." Chris whispered...

"And our Princess started moving..."

"Oh wow!" Chandra exclaimed...

"Sid put his hand on my stomach and she moved over by his hand...

"Aww..." they both said...

"Did you record it?" Chris asked...

"Yea..." I sighed...

"Oh I wanna see that!" Chandra exclaimed...

"No you don't!" Chris and I both exclaimed and then we all bust out laughing...

"Okay – let's get you out of that dress – and into your wedding dress..." Chris said as they helped me out of the dress I was wearing and helped me into my wedding dress...

"Oh my God..." Chris whispered as she started to cry...

"I'm not going to let you ruin my make-up..." I laughed as Chandra dabbed my eyes...

"Alright – Chris – she needs her garter belt – matter fact – put this on her thigh – I'll go get Maui ..."

"Yes Maam..." Chris laughed as she put on my garter belt...

"Hi Maui..." I said...

"This is Maui's dress..." Chris said as she took it out the bag...

"Oh my God – that's so cute!" I exclaimed...

"I don't have any more tissues..." Chandra laughed as she dabbed my eyes. Chris put the dress on Maui and picked her up...

"Are you ready?" Chandra asked...

"Yes..." I sighed...

"Okay ladies – let's go!" Chandra said as we followed her downstairs...

"You look good Sid..." Bazil said...

"Thanks Bazil – you look good too..."

"You ready?"

"I'm ready..."

"Okay – let's go!" Bazil said as they all went downstairs...

"Mommy – look at the dog!" Jay exclaimed as everyone turned around. Maui held a little basket of rose petals in her mouth as she strutted down the aisle followed by Chris and Chandra...

"Aww..." everyone said in unison. I waited for Chris and Chandra to take their place. Maui put the basket down at Sid's feet and sat in front of Chris and Chandra, and then I started walking down the aisle... and when I saw Sid, I couldn't hold back the tears and neither could he...

"I don't have any more tissues..." Chandra whispered as she dabbed my eyes and Sid dabbed his as Darryl began the ceremony...

"Beloved... we are gathered here this afternoon to join Obsidian Heart and Amber Morrison in marriage. You have both come before me and expressed your desire to become husband and wife. Do you have rings?"

"Yes – we have rings..." Bazil said as he took two ring boxes out his pocket...

"Okay – take the rings out the boxes – Amber – you take his ring – Obsidian – you take her ring..."

"Okay..." we both said in unison as I took his ring and he took mine...

"Who gives this woman to be married? Darryl asked...

"I give myself..." I answered...

"Okay – Obsidian – do you have anything you want to say to Amber?"

"Yes I do..." Sid answered as he took my hands...

"Amber, My Queen,

When you walked into my office – I knew there was something special about you. You had a beautiful aura that glowed around you and I felt sad every time you left work. You brightened my world and my heart without effort just by being who you are. I'm so happy you chose me again in this life..."

"Okay – Amber – do you have anything you want to say to Obsidian?"

"Yes I do..." I answered as I took his hands...

"Obsidian, My King,

I was drawn to you from the moment I saw you. I knew I belonged to you before I understood what was happening between us. Whenever I was around you, I felt a surge of energy – and it felt good. I didn't understand it – but I knew I needed it – I knew I needed you. I'm so happy I have a chance to love you again in this life..."

"Okay – Obsidian, Amber – do you have anything you want to say to your Princess?"

"Yes we do..." we answered as we both placed our hands on my stomach...

"Princess,

We love you with all that we are. You are confirmation from God and our elders that we were destined to be together again in this life. We promise to love you more than we love each other and raise you and your brother in a home filled with love and joy..."

"Obsidian – put the ring on Amber's finger and repeat after me..." Darryl said...

"Okay – I'm ready..." Sid said...

"Amber, My Queen,

I take you as my wife, with your faults and your strengths, as I offer myself to you with my faults and my strengths..." Sid repeated after Darryl and then he continued... "I will help you when you need help and turn to you when I need help. Today - I choose to spend the rest of my life with you..." I started crying as Sid repeated the vows to me. When he was finished, I took his face in my hands and kissed him...

"Amber – put the ring on Obsidian's finger and repeat after me..."

"Okay – I'm ready..." I said...

"Obsidian, My King,

I take you as my husband, with your faults and your strengths, as I offer myself to you with my faults and my strengths. I repeated after Darryl and then he continued... "I will help you when you need help and turn to you when I need help. Today – I choose to spend the rest of my life with you..."

"By the power invested in me by the State of Massachusetts and the City of Boston – I now pronounce you husband and wife · Obsidian – you may kiss your bride! Ladies and Gentlemen – I present to you – Mr. & Mrs. Heart!"

"Woo hoo!"

"Yeeaaa!" we heard as we held each other and continued kissing...

"I love you..." Chris breathed as she pulled Chandra into a kiss...

"I love you too..." Chandra breathed as she kissed her...

"Congratulations Darryl said as we all hugged..."

"Congratulations..." Bazil said...

Thank you Bazil..." Sid said...

"Congratulations..." Chris said...

"Congratulations..." Chandra said...

"Congratulations..." Beautiee said as she got up and hugged us both...

"Congratulations!" the kids squealed in unison...

"Thank you all!" Sid exclaimed...

"How soon will we get our marriage certificate?" I asked...

"You'll get it in about a week or so..."

"Thank you Darryl..." I said...

"Thank you Darryl..." Obsidian said...

"You're welcome – now let's get started on your reception!" Darryl yelled as we all followed him into the banquet room...

Chapter 46

Wedding Reception
Friday, May 7th, 2021, 2 p.m.

"My King..." I whispered as I heard 'When I Give My Love To You' playing...

"I love you Mrs. Heart..." Sid whispered as he pulled me into his arms and we danced...

"I love you too Mr. Heart..." I whispered in his ear..."

"I can't wait to get you upstairs..."

"Me either..." Sid held me tighter and I could feel his dick against me...

"You feel that?"

"Yeesss..."

"You want it?"

"Yeeess..." The song was over and we stood in the middle of the floor holding each other and kissing as everyone applauded...

"I love you..."

"I love you too..." Sid pulled me into another kiss and held me as everyone applauded again. Bazil started tapping his champagne glass and everyone else did the same as we continued kissing...

"Come with me Mrs. Heart..." Sid said as he took my hand and led me to the head of the table, pulled out the chair, waited for me to sit down, and then sat down beside me. Bazil sat next to Sid, Beautiee sat next to Bazil, Jay sat next to Beautiee, Joseph sat next to Jay, Joy sat next to Joseph, and Lydia sat next to Joy. Chris sat next to me, Chandra sat next to Chris, and Maui went to lie down in the corner away from the table. A bottle of Prosecco was sitting in the middle of each table and the glasses were already filled. Bazil stood up to speak first...

"Everyone please raise your glass!" everyone raised their glass, including, his children... "To Mr. & Mrs. Heart!" he exclaimed as he took a sip of champagne...

"To Mr. & Mrs. Heart!" everyone said in unison as they all took a sip of champagne...

"I like champagne!" Jay exclaimed as we all laughed...

"I don't..." Joseph said as he shook his head and put the glass down on the table...

"I like it!" Joy exclaimed...

"I don't want anymore..." Lydia said as she shook her head and put her glass back down on the table. We laughed as the waiter came over to the table and replaced their glasses of champagne with sparkling cider...

"I have something I want to say..." Chris said as she stood up... "Amber, we go way back. If I had known way back when we met that I would be the one to help you on this journey, I'd still be here. I love you guys..."

"Aww..." everyone said as we all took another sip and I teared up...

"I love you to Chris..." I said as I stood up and we hugged...

"I love you to Chris..." Sid said as he stood up and went to hug Chris...

"I have something I want to say too..." Beautiee said as she stood up... "Thank you both for allowing me to tell your story and be a part of it..."

"You're welcome..." we both said as we all took another sip...

"I have something I need to say..." Bazil said as he stood up... "Sid – you and Amber brought us back to one of the happiest times in our life – and we'll never forget that. Thank you..."

"You're welcome..." we both said we all took another sip...

"Can I say something?" Jay asked as he stood up...

"Go ahead Jay..." Bazil answered...

"Thank you for inviting us to your wedding..."

"Aww... you're welcome!" we both exclaimed as we all took another sip...

"Sid?" Bazil asked...

"Yes Bazil?"

"There's something we have to do..."

"There is?"

"Yes..." he answered as he got up from the table... "Amber, please stand. I stood up and Bazil pulled my chair into the middle of the room, took me by the hand, and sat me down in the chair. Sid came over to me and smiled at me mischievously as everyone started chanting...

"Take it off! Take it off! Take it off!"

"Well?" I asked...

"Ssshhh..." he whispered and then he bent down to kiss me, squatted down, and pushed my legs open. Thank God my dress was long so nobody could see what was going on as he put his head up under my dress...

"Woo hoo!"

"Yea!"

"Take it off!" Sid kissed his way up my thigh until he reached the garter and then he nibbled on my thigh as he took the garter in his teeth...

"Sid... that tickles..." I laughed as I grabbed his head...

"Save it for later!" Chandra yelled out as everyone laughed and he came out from under my dress with the garter in his teeth, stood up, and took a bow as everyone applauded. Sid put the garter in his pocket, pulled me up out the chair, and kissed me hard...

"Woo hoo!"

"Yea!" Bazil came to get the chair and put it back at the table and waited for me to sit down before we all got ready to eat....

"I need everybody to hold hands..." Sid said. Sid waited for everyone to hold hands and then he stood up, took my hand, and Bazil's hand... "Lord – thank you – for giving me another chance at happiness!"

"Amen!" we all said in unison. We all got up and went to the hors d'oeuvres station as jazz played in the background and I noticed Maui was coming over towards us...

"What's wrong Maui – you hungry?" Chris asked...

"We'll get you something to eat..." Chandra said as Maui sat and waited...

"Here..." the waiter said as he came over to us and handed Chris an aluminum tin...

"Make sure you give Maui some of everything..." I said...

"Yes Amber – we know!" Chris laughed as she filled the tin. Chris took the tin over to the corner and Maui wagged her tail as she ate some of the following hors d'oeuvrs:

Spinach Dip
Marinated Olives
Antipasto Platter,
Assorted Mini Deep Dish Pizzetta
Assorted Miniature Calzones

"I'm surprised the kids like the appetizers..." Beautiee said...

"Ssshhh!" Bazil whispered...

"They are really good..." Sid said...

"They're delicious..." Chris said...

"I hope Maui goes back to eating regular food after this..." Chandra said...

"Everything's really good..." Sid said...

"Did you know about the food when you picked this place?" I asked...

"No — I've just always wanted to come here..." Sid answered...

"I've always wanted to come here too..." I sighed as I pulled him into a kiss...

"Aww..." everyone said in unison...

"The main course is ready..." the waiter said as he came over to the table...

"Jay, Joseph, Joy, Lydia — are you ready to eat some more?" Bazil asked...

"Yeeessss!" they all answered as we got up and went over to the Italian Family Style Station and saw the following:

Roasted Veal Parmesan with
Mariana Sauce over Linguini
Sautéed Chicken Piccata over
Angel Hair Pasta
Shrimp Scampi over
Angel Hair Pasta
Meatballs with Bolognese Sauce
Over Spaghetti

Oven-Roasted Potatoes
Charcoal Grilled Vegetables
Caesar Salad
Caprese Flatbread
Breadsticks
Garlic Bread with Butter

"I'm sorry Amber — Maui can't have all this..." Chris sighed...

"As long as she can have something..." I said as we filled our plates. The waiter came over to Chris and gave her another tin and Chris put some vegetables, potatoes, and sautéed chicken in it and brought it over to Maui...

"Maui sure is lucky today!" Chandra said...

"I'm just happy that she was allowed to be here..." Sid said...

"That was really nice of them — but Maui's so adorable — who could resist?" Beautiee said...

"The kids are having fun with her..." Bazil said...

"Jay, Joseph, Joy, Lidia – make sure you eat..." Beautiee said...

We all went back to the table and continued eating and talking...

"So have you decided where you'll be going on your honeymoon?" Beautiee asked...

"I have..." Sid answered...

"You have?" I asked...

"It's a surprise..."

"Aww..." everyone said...

"What's a honeymoon?" Jay asked...

"A honeymoon is a vacation you take to celebrate that you got married..." Bazil explained...

"I thought this was the celebration..." Joy said...

"This is the wedding and reception..." Joseph explained... "The honeymoon comes after that – right Daddy?"

"That's right..." Bazil answered...

"Did you go on a honeymoon Mommy?" Lydia asked...

"Yes..." Beautiee answered... "We went to Nassau Paradise Island..."

"Ooohhh..." the kids sighed...

"We went to Hawaii..." Chris sighed...

"It was beautiful..." Chandra sighed as they kissed...

"Aww..." we all said in unison...

"We're going on a Grand Tour of Europe from London to Rome and we'll also visit Florence, Italy..." Sid said...

"Oh Sid!" I exclaimed as I started crying...

"We'll be gone for 20 days – we leave on June 18th..."

"I love you so much!" I exclaimed as I pulled him into a kiss...

"I love you too..."

"Aww..." everyone exclaimed. We continued eating and talking until we were finished and then it was time for cake...

"My Queen..."

"Yes My King?"

"Come with me..." he said as he stood up and extended his hand...

"Okay!" I squealed as he took me over to the cake...

"Smash it in his face! Smash it in his face!" everyone yelled...

"Sid... wait a minute..."

"Nope!" he laughed as he took some of the cake off his plate and smashed it in my face as everyone laughed...

"Sid! You got it in my hair!"

"I'm sorry..." he sighed...

"I'm not!" I laughed as I took a piece of cake and smashed it on the side of his face, making sure I got some of the cake and icing in his hair as everyone laughed...

"Come here..." he said as he smiled at me mischievously...

"No..." I laughed...

"I said..." he laughed as he pulled me close to him... "Come here... and open your mouth..." he laughed as he held a small piece of cake in between his fingers...

"Okay... okay..." I laughed as I opened my mouth and he put the cake in my mouth... "Mmmm... it's good... your turn..." I said as I picked up a small piece of cake in between my fingers and held it in front of his mouth...

"Okay... I'ma open my mouth... and you're not gonna smash it on my nose... right?"

"I'm not going to smash your nose..." I laughed...

"Okay..." he laughed as he opened his mouth and I put a piece of cake in his mouth...

"Mmmm..." he said as he pulled me into a kiss and put his tongue in my mouth with cake on it...

"Mmmm..." I moaned...

"You need us to leave?" Bazil asked as everyone laughed...

"You can stay if you want..." Sid laughed as he picked up another piece of cake, held it between his lips, and pulled me into another kiss...

"Aww shit!"

"Woo hoo!"

"C'mon – let's let everyone get a piece of cake..." he laughed as we went back to the table...

"I've never had cake like that before..." I laughed...

"Me either..."

"I wanna do it again..."

"Are you ready to go My Queen?" he asked as he smiled at me mischievously...

"Yes My King... I'm ready..."

"May I have everyone's attention?" Sid asked as he stood up. Sid waited for everyone to be quiet and then he continued... "Thank you all for coming and celebrating with us. We're going to go get comfortable and get ready for tonight..." he said as he took me by the hand and walked me out the dining room...

"Well then – I'll guess we'll go walk Maui and then we'll go get comfortable too..." Chris said as she got up along with Chandra...

"I'm glad we're staying here – I'm tired – I can't wait to go lie down and relax..." Beautiee said...

"Yes... Relax..." Bazil said as they all laughed...

"Do you think they know?" I asked...

"I'm sure they know..." Sid laughed...

"I sure hope these walls aren't too thin..."

"Their room is at one end of the hall – our room is at the other end of the hall – I think we'll be fine..." Sid said as he picked me up in his arms, opened the door, and carried me into our room...

"Mommy – can we play with Maui?" Joy asked...

"You need to ask Chris and Chandra..." Beautiee said...

"Can we play with Maui? Please?" Joy asked...

"Sure – we'll bring her to your room after we take her for a walk..." Chris answered...

"Yeaaaa!" she squealed as they all ran to their room...

"I hope you're not too tired..." Bazil said as he pulled Beautiee into a kiss...

"I'm not tired at all..." Beautiee said as she smiled at him mischievously...

Chapter 47

**Wedding Night
Friday, May 7th, 2021, 8 p.m.**

"My Queen..."
"Yes My King..."

"It's time..." he breathed as he kissed me...

"It's time..." I breathed...

"It's all be leading up to this moment..." he breathed in my ear as he slid my dress of my shoulders and let it fall to the floor...

"Yeesss..." I whispered...

"And now..." he breathed as he unhooked my bustier and slid it off my breasts... "You will submit to me..." he breathed as he began kissing me on my neck while sliding my thong down...

"Yesss..." I whispered again...

"You're shaking..."

"I know..." I said as he stepped back away from me...

"Undress me..." he commanded...

"Yes My King..." I breathed as I pushed his jacket off his shoulders. Sid stood still as I unbuttoned his shirt and pushed it off his shoulders... "Lift your arms..." I commanded. Sid lifted his arms and when I pulled his shirt off, I began kissing his chest as I unbuckled his belt and slid his pants and boxers off his ass..."

"No!" he growled as he pulled me close to him and kissed me hard...

"Please..." I breathed. Sid grabbed my shoulders and gripped them as I dropped down to my knees...

"Yessss..." he breathed as he felt my lips on his dick. I deliberately took my time kissing around the head of his dick and down his shaft as he played in my hair...

"Ooohhh..." he moaned as I took his dick in my mouth. When I stopped he looked at me as if he was confused... "Why'd you..."

"Sshh..." I whispered as I put my finger on his mouth, got on the bed, and got on my back...

"I'm going to punish you..." he growled as he grabbed my legs, hoisted me up, and thrust himself inside me...

"Oh Sid... Fuck!" I cried out...

"Ugh! Ugh! Ugh!" he growled as he held me by my waist and pounded me standing up...

"Haah! Haah! Haah!" I screamed...

"I warned you!!" he growled as he continued pounding me...

"Haah! Haah! Haah!"

"Ugh! Ugh! Ugh!

"My Kiinnnggg! I'm cumming!"

"Cum for your King!!"

"Haaahhh!!!"

"Get on your knees!!" he commanded. I got up, turned around, got on my knees, and my legs began to tremble as he spread my ass cheeks...

"Aaaah!" I cried out as he thrust himself inside me again...

"Yes! Give it to me!" he growled as he slammed his dick inside me...

"Haah... My King... Fuck... I'm cumming again! Aaah! Aah! Aaah!"

"Get on your back!!" he commanded. I got on my back and Sid came to bed and lay down beside me... "Are you ready?"

"I don't understand..." I panted...

"Are you ready for me?"

"Yes My King – Yes!" I breathed. Sid got up on top of me and, to my surprise; he eased himself inside me...

"I'm going to ask you again..." he breathed as he pushed himself in deeper... "Are you ready?"

"Yes My King!" I moaned. Sid brought both my legs up, braced them on his shoulders, lay down on top of me, and pushed his tongue in my mouth as he fucked me hard... "Hmmph! Hmmph! Hmmph!"

"Ummph! Ummph! Ummph!" he moaned as he pushed himself in deeper. Sid grabbed the headboard and rocked me underneath him as I exploded...

"HMMPH! HMMPH! HMMPH! HMMPH!"

"UGH! UGH! UGH! UUUGGGHHH!!" I grabbed his ass and Sid released the headboard and wrapped his arms under me as we continued kissing...

"Sorry about that Princess..." I panted...

"Why are you apologizing to our daughter?" he laughed...

"Because I think you scared the shit out of her..." I laughed...

"Sorry Princess..." he laughed...

"Are you ready My King?" I asked as I pushed him down on his back and straddled him...

"Yes My Queen – Yessss!" he moaned as I sat on his dick. I took Sid's hands, locked my fingers with his, and pushed against his hands as he pushed himself up inside me...

"Ooohhh..." I moaned...

"Yes... That's it... Ride it!!"

"Harder..." I moaned....

"As you wish My Queen!!" he growled as he grabbed my hips and thrust himself up inside me deeper...

"My King... Haah..." I moaned as I threw my head back...

"Ugh! Ugh! Ugh!"

"My King! Don't Stop! I'm cumming again!"

"Cum for your King!" he growled...

"Haah! Haah! Haah! Haah!"

"Ugh! Ugh! Ugh! Ugh! Uuuggghhh!"

"What the hell did those crystals and spheres do to us?" I panted...

"You mean what did they do to you..."

"Me?"

"I told you – I've been holding back..."

"I guess I was too..."

"Are you ready?"

"Huh?"

"Get on your back..."

"Yes My King!" I breathed as I got on my back. Sid got up, moved down between my legs, pushed my legs apart, and dove in...

"AAAAH! AAAH! AAAH!"

Chapter 48

"Jade Dulberg please report to the visiting area..." the warden said over the loud speaker...

"Hmmm – Joel's got a full calendar today – it can't be him – I wonder who's coming to see me?" she said as she hurried to the visiting area, sat down, and waited...

"Hi Jade..." Beautiee greeted...

"Umm... Okay... Beautiee... why are you here?"

"I'm here because I want to publish your story..."

"Bitch bye!" Jade laughed as she got up to leave...

"Wait!!" Beautiee exclaimed...

"Why?!" Jade snapped...

"Sit down... please..."

"Okay – I'm sitting..."

"I'm here because I want to publish your story..."

"You already have my story!" Jade laughed...

"I have your husband's story..."

"Isn't that the same thing?"

"Not at all..."

"I'm listening..."

"My readers know Sid's side – but my readers want to know your side..."

"Really?"

"Absolutely – I want to tell your story – from your point of view – I want my readers to know what happened to you – I want to let my readers know where you are now – I see you got married..."

"Yes..."

"See?! That's a story!! You did what you did – you get convicted – you go to prison – and your story continues!!"

"You just want to make money off of me – I'm not stupid!!"

"I know you're not stupid – that's why I'm here..."

"Huh?!"

"Somebody's going to tell your story – let me help you tell your story – I want my readers to know you both had a happy ending..."

"Hmmm – I have nothing but time... I guess I could write a book – I don't know where to start though..."

"I was thinking you could start with this..." Beautiee said as she pulled out a lap top, turned it on, pulled up the cover, and showed it to Jade...

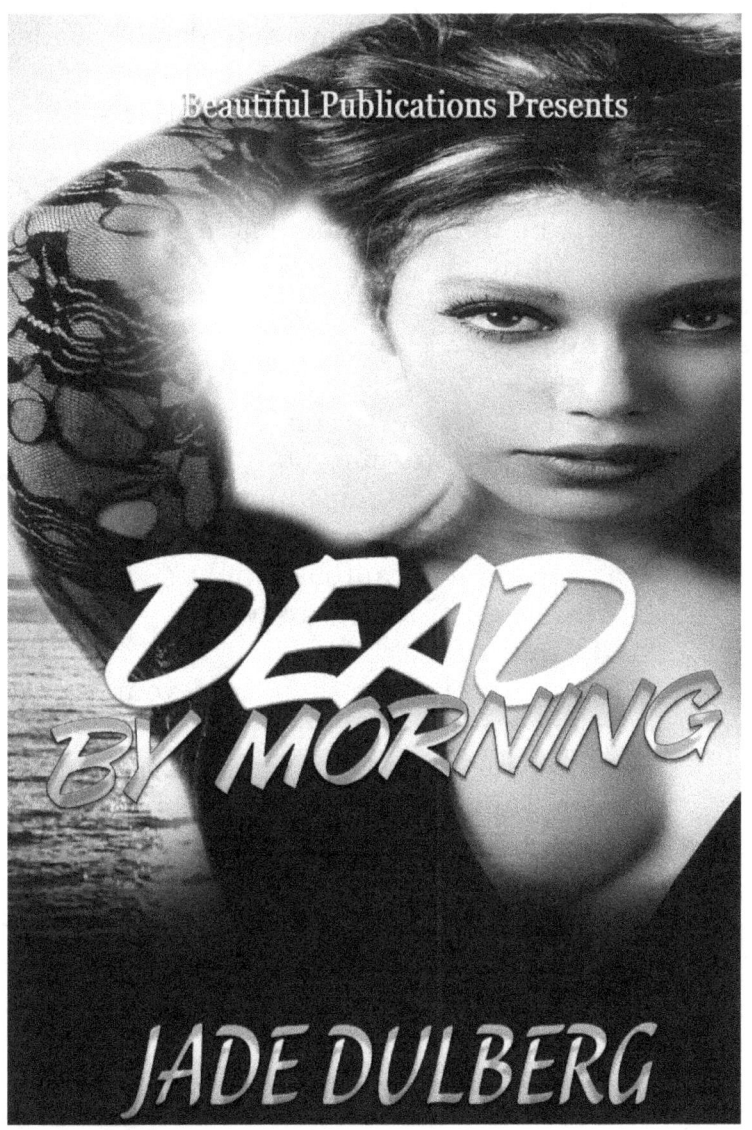

Beautiful Publications Presents

DEAD
BY MORNING

JADE DULBERG

"It's nice – but I'm not dead!" Jade laughed...

"Look at the cover again..." Beautiee said...

"Okay – I'm looking at it..."

"The title isn't about you being dead – it's about you rising from your circumstances – you're coming up through the horizon in spite of everything you've been through – the sun is shining behind you..."

"Oh wow – you're good..."

"I had a conversation with my cover designer – I told him about you – I gave him the title, and this is what he came up with..."

"Why can't we just make the title Jade Dulberg and make it an autobiography?"

"It will be an autobiography..."

"With that title?"

"The title will draw them in – your name and the synopsis will keep them in..."

"Are you sure about this?"

"As you said – I want to make money..."

"That's true – you wouldn't do it if you didn't make money..."

"Trust me – readers will see a book by you and they'll want to read it..."

"Can we put a sub-title underneath it?"

"Like what?"

"Dead By Morning – The Jade Heart Story..."

"I don't think a subtitle is a good idea..."

"Why not?"

"I think you should keep the title and use your married name as the author..."

"How will people know it's me?"

"This is how they'll know..." Beautiee answered as she showed Jade the synopsis...

Dead By Morning Synopsis

"Dead By Morning is Jade Heart's story. In this autobiography, you'll see how Jade rose from the ashes, how she came up through the horizon, and how she was given a second chance at happiness..."

"Okay – I'll do it!!"

"I have a contract here – you can have your attorney look it over before you sign it if you want..."

"Oh wow – Smalls is going to love this!!"

"Did you say Smalls?"

"Yes – why?"

"I'm Beautiee Osgood..."

"I don't get it..."

"I'm Bazil's wife..."

"Oh shit!" Jade exclaimed and then they both bust out laughing...

Chapter 49

One Year Later

"Sid!"

"Wha... What's wrong?" he asked sleepily..."

"The crystals – the spheres..."

"What about them?" he yawned as he sat up...

"They're gone..."

"Gone?!" he exclaimed

"Maybe they're in the kitchen..." I said as I put on my robe and slippers...

"I'll come with you..." he said as he put on his robe and slippers. We went down the hall and I heard Princess cooing so I peeked in her room...

"Sid! Get the phone!" I whispered...

"Okay!" Sid hurried to get his phone and hurried back to me... "Look!"

"Oh my God... that's beautiful..." he whispered as he started recording...

"She's so happy..." I whispered...

"Yes... she is..."

"I wonder how long they've been going in her room..."

"Since we brought her home..."

"How do you know?"

"My mother told me they did the same thing when I was born..."

"We're going to have to keep your son and daughter together..." I said as I rubbed my stomach...

"Why?"

"Your daughter might cry if the crystals and spheres stop going in her room..."

"I wouldn't worry about that..." he said as he came up behind me and wrapped his arms around my stomach...

"I love you My King..."

"I love you My Queen..." he breathed in my ear and then he put the phone in his picket, turned me around, opened my robe, grabbed my ass with both hands, pulled me to him, and kissed me hard...

Conversation with My Character, Jade

"Hello..." I greeted as I opened the door for Jade...

"Thank you for agreeing to speak to me..." Jade said...

"You're welcome – let's go sit out on the deck..."

"Wow ‐ you have a nice collection of crystals..."

"Thank you..."

"I'm beginning to understand why you wrote Obsidian's story..." she said as she followed me into the dining room...

"It's not just his story – it's our story..." I said as I opened the door to the deck and we went to sit outside...

"True – but I'm not here to talk about Sid – I'm here to talk about you... and me..."

"Why'd you want to speak to me?" I asked, as if I didn't already know the answer...

"You know damn well why I wanted to speak to you!" she snapped...

"Watch your tone Jade..."

"Oh – that's right – you like to kill your characters..." she said as she rolled her eyes...

"Keep that up and I'll write a part 3 and your happy ending won't be so happy..."

"I'm sorry Tracy – I didn't mean it like that..."

"Apology accepted..."

"Thank you – I'm here because I don't understand why you didn't kill me – especially when I killed you in a past life and tried to kill you in this one..."

"I never had any intention of killing you – my intent was to tell a drama filled story of crystals, gemstones, spheres, psychics, past lives, and chakras. I started the story with the intent to write my friend Chris and her wife into it – but after I did the readings and discovered that our lives ended tragically, I had to mix it up, create drama, and keep my readers on the edge of their seats..."

"I still don't get why you didn't kill me..."

"Well damn – did you really wanna die?" I laughed...

"Of course not – I just figured that's where you'd go – it's not like I didn't deserve to die – I did try and kill you - again..." she laughed...

"Yes you did – but I wanted my readers to understand what you were feeling..."

"Especially since you stole my husband's heart..." she laughed...

"He was husband first!" I laughed...

"Yes - he was your husband in a past life – and now he's your husband in this life..."

"Yes he is..." I sighed...

"Why'd you give me a happy ending? Why didn't you let me rot in prison?"

"You'll do your time – but I felt you deserved another chance to be happy – if I didn't come back to drop off the key you wouldn't've tried to kill me..."

"I thought your friend Chris said you were supposed to be there?"

"I was – but what if I waited until the next day?"

"Then I might've gotten out in 7 years instead of 12..." she sighed...

"Exactly..."

"Are you going to write a part 3 and let everyone see us living happily ever after?"

"No..."

"Okay..." she laughed... "I tried it - thanks for not killing me..." she said as she got up...

"How's your husband?"

"He's as good as you can get in prison..." she laughed...

"Good..."

"Alright – I'll see myself out..." she said as she got up...

"I'll let you out..." I said...

"Relax – it's a nice day – I'll walk..." she said as she walked through the backyard, down the driveway, and then she disappeared.